FOR THOSE ABOUT TO READ, WE SALUTE YOU!

About the Spartapuss series...

'Cattastic' – London Evening Standard

'Non-stop adventure... Spartapuss serves notice that cattitude rules!' – I Love Cats (USA)

'It's Rome AD36 and the mighty Feline Empire rules the world. This is the diary of slave cat Spartapuss, who finds himself imprisoned and sent off to gladiator school to learn how to fight, for fight he must if he wants to win his freedom. Packed with more catty puns than you ever thought pawsible, this witty Roman romp is history with cattitude.' – Scholastic Junior Magazine

'Spartapuss makes history fun instead of dull...For people who don't like history (like me), this book might change their minds.' – Shruti Patel, aged 10

'...the descriptions of life in classical Rome are good, particularly the set piece in the Arena...Readers who know the original stories will enjoy the fun, and those who don't know the history may be enticed to look more closely at the Roman stories.' – The School Librarian

'I really enjoyed this book and I liked the fact that it was written as if it was Spartapuss's diary. My favourite character was Russell (a crow!!!) Spartapuss's friend. I would recommend this book for ages 10+ especially if you enjoy books with a twist and a sense of humour.'
– Sam (11-year-old Young Archaeologist member from York)

'A truly hilarious story... One of the UK's brightest new authors.' ... 'A must read for children and cat lovers'.
– Teaching and Learning Magazine

'Two paws up! A stylish, witty and thoroughly engaging tale that will captivate young and old readers alike.'
– Tanuja Desai Hidier, author of 'Born Confused'
(Winner of the London Writer's Award for Fiction 2001)

'...a unique couple of books that have really caught the imagination of the public here... clearly something special.' – Andrew Fairmaner (buyer, The British Museum)

'This fantastic tale of the Roman Empire ruled by cats is a must for children and adults alike... This is a really fantastic tale! With another three in the series, there's more adventure to come.' – Sarah, Ottakar's East Grinstead

'Catligula's reign, a time when cats ruled Rome, was short if bloody, a story told by freedcat Spartapuss, employed as a scribe by Catligula, whose life was saved by Spartapuss. The Emperor is mad, poisoning those he believes to be his enemies and making his pet, Rattus Rattus, a member of the Senate. The Spraetorian Guard are determined to end his reign before Catligula ruins the empire.

Based loosely upon the writings of classical historians, Catligula is the second in a series that re-tells the scandals of the early Caesars in an accessible form, inevitably reminiscent of Robert Graves' *I, Claudius*. The jokes lie mainly in the names – the Greeks become Squeaks – but the descriptions of life in classical Rome are good, particularly the set piece in the Arena, when Catligula plays himself in what must have been an embarrassing display to even his sycophantic feline audience.

Readers who know the original stories will enjoy the fun, and those who don't know the history may be enticed to look more closely at the Roman stories.'

– The School Librarian, Vol 53 no 4, 2005

CATLIGULA

ROBIN PRICE

MOGZILLA

CATLIGULA

First published by Mogzilla in 2005
Second printing June 2006.

ISBN 10: 0-9546576-1-6
ISBN 13: 978-0-9546576-1-1

Copyright © 2005 Robin Price
Cover illustration by Phil Hall
Cover copyright © Mogzilla 2005
Cover layout and typesetting: Surface Impression
Copy editor: Annabel Else
Spartapuss and Catligula are registered trade marks.

www.mogzilla.co.uk

Printed in the UK

The author would like to thank the following
people (and their friends) for all of their help and
encouragement:
Michele, Peter, Hayley, Christina G, Sam, Phil,
Annabel, Rupert, Nick, Ricky, John G, Sinc, Andrew,
Bev, Les, Kirsty, Claire E, Twiz, Ed, Arvind, Tanuja,
Bernard, Jon, Olivia, Am, Ben, David, Mum and
Dad, Nicole, Catherine B, Nicholas R, Guy G,
Caroline C and Rupert.

For Scarlet...

THE TALE SO FAR...

CATLIGULA is the second book in the SPARTAPUSS series. It is set in ancient Rome in a world ruled entirely by cats, where humans have never existed.

In I AM SPARTAPUSS, the first book in the series, Spartapuss is comfortable managing Spatopia, Rome's finest Bath and Spa. He is a loyal servant to his master Clawdius – a cat of the Imperial Family.

But Fortune has other plans for him. There is a nasty incident in the vomitorium. It causes offence to Gattus Tiberius, (nicknamed 'Catligula') the would-be heir to the cushioned throne. Spartapuss is thrown into prison, only to be released into Gladiator training school. He fights at the Games and is freed by Catligula. This makes Clawdius angry, for he has now lost a valuable slave. Shortly afterwards, Spartapuss rescues Catligula from the wreckage of a chariot crash.

In CATLIGULA, the second book in the series, Spartapuss finds himself free, but unemployed.

DRAMATIS PAWSONAE
Who's who!

From the deserts of Fleagypt to the forests of Purrmania, The Feline Empire rules the known world.

Cats of the Imperial Family:

Tiberius – Rome's aging Emperor. Nickname: 'Tibbles'
'Catligula' – real name Gattus Tiberius. Next in line for the cushioned throne
Clawdius – Catligula's uncle. Owner of Spatopia, 'Rome's Finest Bath and Spa' and Spartapuss' ex-master
Mogullania – Clawdius' wife

Cats of the military:

Captain Matro – head of the Spraetorian guard
Dogren of Purrmania – chief of the Emperor's Bodyguards, commonly known as 'the Purrmanians'

Slaves, freedcats, strays and other animals:

Spartapuss – ex-manager of Spatopia, recently freed but now unemployed
Russell – a crow. A good friend of Spartapuss
Katrin – a cook at Spatopia
Neferkitti – a cleaner at the Imperial Palace
Tefnut – a mystic

Find out more at www.mogzilla.co.uk

APURILIS XII
April 12th

It's been a while since I've written this diary of mine, but now I will take pen to paw once again. I must get some scribing practice ready for my first day at the Imperial Palace tomorrow. It'll be an early start, so I have ordered a bowl of roasted chicken for breakfast. I expect that the cook has begun to drown it in vinegar sauce already. Here at Bathhausia, they claim to be 'Rome's most authentic Purrmanian-themed Bath and Spa'. They have been very good to let me have a room but believe me, you can go too far with a theme. I have no clue what the cook put in last night's special – the Black Dumplings of the Forest Worker. They tasted delicious, but this morning I felt sick at the smell of my own breath. I've been eating grass all day.

I dare not risk bear's breath tomorrow, for I must make a good impression. I confess that I am not entirely sure about my new job. If anyone else tells me that 'The Imperial Palace is a nest of vipers!' I'll chew my tail off with worry. I plan to keep my mouth shut and my ears open and write everything down in this diary. Luckily, I have got hold of a slightly longer scroll this time, so there is plenty of room for any gossip or palace scandal that I happen to overhear.

FREEDOM'S PRICE

How is it that I, Spartapuss, was called to work at the Imperial Palace? I will begin my tale with yesterday's events. I was pawing the sauce off my cod breakfast when a messenger arrived. He was better dressed than the average messenger and Mewpiter be praised, he did not mark before he entered. With a yawn, he explained that he'd been told to wait while I read the letter and take my reply back to the sender. I had been dreading this for weeks. I don't like arguments, but I am in the middle of a nasty one. It's with Clawdius, the owner of Spatopia - 'Rome's most popular Bath and Spa' according to their advertising. He is a cat of the Imperial Family and he was once my master. When I won my freedom at a Gladiator fight at the Games of Purrcury, Clawdius' first action was to cancel my Spa membership, sending me a short letter saying only: 'Congratulations. Freedom has a high price!'

He was right about that. You have to buy your own food and collars for a start. And don't let the shopkeepers know you're a freedcat because they'll double the price of everything.

For my part, I dearly wish that Clawdius and I could get on like we did before Catligula made him free me at the Games. It is said that you never forget your first master and so against my friends' advice, I wrote to tell him so. A month later, I got a letter back from his wife, Mogullania, with a bill for fifty gold coins. She called it an 'administration fee' for setting me free.

ALL RIGHT MNIAOW

As I opened the letter, I said a little prayer to Paws. He is known as the God of War but he also does silly disagreements. I was praying that Clawdius would come around to my way of thinking. As soon as the messenger gave me the letter, I knew it was unusual. For one thing, Clawdius never writes on new paper. He has been known to stay up all night long, rubbing out old scrolls so that he can tear them up and use them again, as shopping lists for his wife Mogullania. When I caught a whiff of the scent on the letter, I knew that it was not from Clawdius.

> Spartapuss,
>
> Meet me at the Imperial garden at noon. My messenger will show you the way. There is nothing to fear. You will learn something that is very much in your interest.
>
> Matro,
> Captain of The Spraetorian guard

This was most unexpected. The Spraetorians police the city and guard the Imperial Family. I certainly didn't want to get off on the wrong paw with them.

As I read the letter for the second time, the messenger, who said his name was Mniaow, was busy exploring my bookshelves. When I called to get his attention

I startled him and he knocked a bowl from the shelf. It smashed into tiny pieces. Lucky it wasn't a fine one because, under Bathhausia Rule XIV, the customer must pay for all breakages. I told him that it was all right. I could always ask the cleaners to bury it in their waste pit. Mniaow didn't apologise.

"Well?" he said impatiently. "What is your answer?"

"Oh dear," I said. "I suppose I'd better go with you. But I have no clue what your master can want with me."

"Captain Matro's not my master," said Mniaow.

"I'm sorry," I said. "No offence meant."

"None taken freedcat," he replied. "When offence is taken, you will know it. I'm here on this errand because I owe Matro one. More than one actually. I must have offended Fortune herself! We were playing at mice last night and Captain Matro licked me clean."

"My mother always used to say that 'If you lose at gambling you must be sure to keep on playing until you win it all back.'," I said.

Mniaow smiled. For the first time since he arrived he gave me his full attention.

"Thank your mother for that advice," he said. "And since you've asked for mine, you should smarten yourself up a bit. Just because you were once a slave, doesn't mean you have to go wearing that old wooden monstrosity around your neck for the rest of your life. Didn't your mother ever tell you, 'Look the part and you'll get the job'?"

As it happened that was not one of her sayings. There was one about avoiding the job, but I cannot now remember it. Following Mniaow's advice, I took off my wooden collar – the symbol of the freed Gladiator and put it away carefully in its case.

"Now I will dress you for the palace," said Mniaow.

And he began to turn the room upside down looking for the right outfit. Something fell from a box and caught his eye – my golden coin. It was a good luck present from my teacher at gladiatorial school. The gold is Fleagyptian, ancient but still bright. It is the only thing of value that I own.

Mniaow attached it to a simple leather collar and fastened it around my neck.

"Perfect!" he said. "Now you look acceptable." And he stalked off in the direction of the palace.

THE OLD CAMPAIGNERS

Steps, I hate them. Why the builders insist on putting them everywhere, I do not know. One of the city planners must have got a geometry set for his birthday and amused himself drawing lots of neat squares. From Bathhausia to the Imperial Palace is an hour's journey. I am not now as fit as I was after weeks of Gladiator training and I'm ashamed to say that I was puffing by the time we reached the palace gates. After a word with Mniaow, the Spraetorians who guard the East Gate opened their oak barrier and let us through. Two of them padded over to escort us towards the Imperial gardens for my meeting with their captain.

The Spraetorians are the only soldiers allowed within the city walls, except for the Emperor's Purrmanian Bodyguards. That makes the commander of the Spraetorians one of the most powerful cats in all of Rome. I had no clue what he wanted with me.

The first guard coughed and spat. He was a wiry looking tabby who looked as if his sixteen years of military service were nearly up. Soon he'd be collecting his pension and his cushion of service. He was lean from years on military rations – dried fish and drier biscuits, plus whatever pickings you can loot whilst 'on campaign'. But the Spraetorians rarely go on campaign like the other legions. It is their job to police Rome and guard the Emperor, whilst everyone else is off conquering and looting and having fun. Maybe that's why they always look so hard done by.

The second guard sprang at a passing butterfly. Like us, it was making its way towards the Emperor's kitchen garden. It was quite some leap for a small cat. With an accurate swipe, he batted the unfortunate insect to the ground and trod it into the dust without breaking stride. He didn't even bother to stop and eat it. What is it about guards? Is there something about the uniform that attracts the ill-tempered? Our two guards seemed worried about something. I decided that the military life was not for me. Whatever Captain Matro wanted, I would look for a way to say no without getting his hackles up.

THE BELL

The guards escorted us to a quiet garden, behind the palace kitchens. It was beautifully kept with herbs growing, a private fishpond and vegetables planted in what looked like a tortoise formation. Apparently, the gardener is a retired Spraetorian. At the far end of the garden stands an ancient cedar tree, at the entrance to the Emperor's park.

Later, I learned that this kitchen garden was a favourite spot of the Emperor Augustpuss, who would sleep by the pool and sit up in the tree as night fell, thinking about his great battles in the land of Purrmania and other important matters of state.

It was a peaceful place all right but with each step into the garden, my two escorts became more wary. Although we were still in the palace grounds it was as if they knew they were trespassing on someone else's territory. Without warning, we halted under the big cedar tree and they began to whisper to each other. Mniaow flicked his tail. Then a great crash shook the cedar's branches. I heard snarls. Then the sound of a jangling collar bell, like the sort that the infectious must wear in hospital.

"I'm late for a costume fitting, I must fly," said Mniaow. He pretended not to hear the bell but of course we all heard it. Something unclean was out there. Without waiting for a reply Mniaow charged back towards the palace. At the same moment, I saw a movement in the bushes ahead of me. An old Spraetorian shot towards us like a javelin. His coat was thick with leaves and his ears were bleeding where they'd been torn by the Emperor's thorn bushes. I heard the ringing again. Someone had hung a brass bell around his neck. The three of us backed away, sniffing the air. I must admit that I have always had a horror of catching a terrible disease, like the mange.

"Purrmanians! Purrmanians! Run lads. They are almost upon us!" shouted the stranger.

BLACK FOREST CATS HO!

The fierceness of the Purrmanians has passed into legend. Mothers still tell their kittens, 'Behave yourself, or we'll leave you up a tree in the Black Forest for the Purrmanians.' Rome has been at war with the barbarian tribes of Purrmania since history began. No one can remember exactly who started the wars but all here agree that it was the Purrmanians' fault, for straying into our territory. Captives from the wars were brought back to Rome and displayed in great triumphs at the Arena. Romans love a good triumph. Because of their impressive size, some of the Purrmanian fighters who survived the Games were chosen for bodyguard duties. There have been Purrmanians guarding Roman Emperors ever since. Although it is also the Spraetorians' job to guard our Emperor, in troubled times nine out of ten Emperors have preferred two lines of defence.

DOGREN OF PURRMANIA

The escaped prisoner shot up the cedar tree and was soon lost in its green canopy. The two Spraetorian guards and I stood rooted to the ground as we watched to see what was coming towards us through the trees.

Despite his great bulk, Dogren of Purrmania didn't crash into the clearing, snapping branches and uprooting small trees with his great paws (which were bigger than serving bowls).

Dogren had been born in the Neuterberger Forest, and he knew how to run fast through the trees without making a noise. His tribe, the Kati, had always enjoyed sports. Especially sports that involve a lot of physical contact. Their most popular sport was ambushing Roman legions in their dark forest and giving them a good mauling. In fact, the very name of the Neuterberger Forest was enough to put soldiers off their dried biscuits. Not that they needed much putting off on that account.

How the legions ever managed to capture Dogren remains a closely guarded military secret, so there was obviously some trickery involved. The last time I'd seen Dogren was at the gladiatorial school, where he'd been training Furasians for Father Felinius. The Father had named him 'Dogren' because of his size. He looks more dog than cat. The Emperor Tibbles had appointed him head of the Purrmanian Bodyguards after the last candidate had gone mad. The less said about that the better.

His companion was also huge, and also a

Purrmanian, for all of the Emperor's Bodyguards come from that land. But he was not from the Kati tribe and had not been born in a forest. The trees shook as he crashed into the clearing, forcing his way through the undergrowth as he ran after his prey.

COWARD'S WAY

I looked at the Spraetorian guards. Would they stand and fight? Or would they take the coward's route and follow their comrade up the tree? The old campaigner looked battle-hardened, but he was lean and wiry. No doubt the Spraetorians were well trained, but they were no match for the big Purrmanians. But if Fortune willed it, good sense would prevail. Perhaps the two groups of soldiers had a healthy respect for each other's traditions? Perhaps they worked in co-operation to keep the Emperor safely guarded at all times? I was about to find out.

"Which way did he go?" asked the big Purrmanian. His Catin was perfect and he had hardly a hint of an accent for he had been born in Rome to Purrmanian parents and he'd lived in the capital all his life.

"What's that Chief?" said the old Spraetorian, pricking up an ear.

"Which way did the prisoner go?" said the Purrmanian.

"Vich vay dit zee prizoner go?" repeated the old Spraetorian in a puzzled voice, tilting his head sideways for good measure. His friend laughed.

"There is a problem with our communication. He does not understand what I am saying Sir," said the Purrmanian.

"He is mocking you," growled Dogren in a voice that would worry sheep.

And he took two paces forward and stuck out a paw the size of a gatepost. It connected and the unfortunate Spraetorian toppled like a falling statue.

A DOOMED SPRING

The second Spraetorian thought about it. When there was a fight, his father had always told him to go for the biggest bully. Put the big one down and then you'll win the respect of the rest. He'd also been told to fight with street-rules. Forget squaring up to your opponent and all of that 'I challenge you to a fight!' nonsense that you see in the theatre. Just make sure you get the first blow in. Bite them where it'll make their eyes water, or better still, go for their eyes. So the Spraetorian padded straight up to Dogren and sprang, claws reaching for the eyes.

Dogren smiled. He had won over two hundred fights before his retirement from the Arena. During this time, he'd seen the fashions come and go. There had been pitched battles, death matches, free-fur-alls, female against male, water fights and killing in costumes. Dogren had seen every attack in the book. He'd seen so many attacks, in fact, that he'd rewritten the book and published a new version of it. Sometimes, he used to entertain his friends by reading aloud out from it at parties in his deep growling voice. Some of his friends had bought two or three copies each.

As the Spraetorian sprang towards him, Dogren knew that he was under attack from a quickly improvised combination of the 'Surprise spring' (move XIII) and an aggressive lunge (move IV) 'Claws to the eyes'.

He had to give his Spraetorian opponent some credit for bravery. It was just a shame that it was combined with so much stupidity. With a swift turn Dogren shifted his considerable weight onto his left paw and swung his great body around. This sent the unfortunate Spraetorian flying over his shoulder. He smacked into the trunk of the great cedar tree. The tree shook to its roots. A strange ringing sound came from a spot somewhere high in the branches. Dogren's eyes wandered up the trunk of the great tree. There was nothing to see, save for a cloud of branches covered in dark green needles. Seizing his chance, the Spraetorian remembered his father's other piece of advice and ran off towards the palace, as fast as Purrcury's fiery chariot. His old friend, who had only just regained consciousness, ran after him.

I, CLIMBER

The two Purrmanians stood staring up at the cedar tree. The trunk was huge, but the branches in the middle looked rather thin. A thought occurred to me.

The Emperor's Bodyguards didn't look like born climbers. Dogren had been an accomplished tree climber in his youth, in the Neuterberger Forest. But by the time he was just two years old, he was already getting too heavy. As Fortune spun it, his tribe of the Katimungus had an arrangement with another tribe - the Scati, who would do all their difficult climbing for them in return for protection. The Scati were smaller and more agile. They'd go up the trees and flush out the prey, whilst the big Katimungus bruisers waited below, sharpening their claws. The two Purrmanians turned towards me. For Peus' sake! I thought. I knew what was coming next.

"Climb the tree and we will give you gold," said the first Purrmanian, whose name was Wulf.

I played for time.

"Er, I'm not sure about that. I'm not very brave. What crime did the prisoner commit?"

"He said that he was after songbirds in the Emperor's garden but there are unanswered questions. His story may be false, so we must ask him some more questions before we can come to the correct decision," said Wulf, who was an open-minded cat.

"He is a spy!" growled Dogren, "An assassin, after the Emperor!"

And he wondered what they were teaching them on Bodyguards training these days. Wulf would believe everything anyone told him. Spies and assassins weren't going to hold their paws up and shout 'In the name of Mewpiter, I confess my crimes!' were they?

"A spy!" I gasped, sounding terrified, which was easy.

"He sounds dangerous. He's probably armed."

"He is armed only with a little knifc. Gct him to come down and we will do the rest. We have practised operations like this many times in training. Do not be afraid, there is nothing to fear," said Wulf.

Dogren sighed and gave Wulf a hard stare. "There is nothing to fear!" he said to himself in a furious voice. How in the name of Klaws the Terrible was Wulf going to force me to climb the tree if I had nothing to fear?

"I'd love to help, except I've got a medical problem," I said. "Weak paws you see and a nasty case of lock claw. I'm not good at climbing difficult trees like this. Hiding in bushes would be a different matter. But I could go and find a long ladder for you. I'm sure there'll be one in the kitchen."

"You will climb now!" ordered Dogren in a voice that was usually obeyed.

"I, Dogren, have spoken my word," he added.

"And once he has spoken his word, he will not speak it again," said Wulf, in support of his commander. Dogren sighed again.

I started to back away from the tree. Dogren let out a low growl.

"Just taking a run up," I explained.

I padded back a few more paces. Then I remembered my gladiatorial training. I turned and ran away as fast as I could. Whatever Captain Matro had to tell me, it wasn't worth facing down a cornered Spraetorian for, even if he was only armed with a small knife.

"After him you stuffed sausage!" shouted Dogren.

ANGRY LIKE THE WULF

Far from being a stuffed sausage, Wulf ran like Purrcury himself. He looked too bulky to be a natural runner, but he was surprisingly fast over short distances. As for me, Bathhausia's Black Sausage breakfasts had taken their toll. Soon I started to puff and blow. Wulf was gaining on me. He trained every day for this kind of chase and now he was really enjoying himself.

"Aaaaaarghhh! I eat Kittons' feet!" he shouted.

He was fit enough to shout and run at the same time.

Distracted, I tripped over a tree root and fell nose first into a rotting pile of lemons. The smell made me cough and spit.

Before I knew it, Wulf had grabbed me, stuffed me into a sack and dragged me back to Dogren. There was some shouting. They stopped shouting and talked for a while in the Purrmanian language. Then I was tipped out of the sack.

"We have agreed that we will give you one more chance," said Wulf, slightly embarrassed. "But you must climb the tree this time my friend, or it will go very badly for you. And there will be no gold for you, either!"

Dogren let out a deep growl. What in the name of their forefathers' ruffs was Wulf playing at?

There was nothing for it. So I took a long run up and sprang up the trunk, not daring to stop for breath until I'd reached the first of the lowest branches.

HAIL CEDAR!

Cedars have stood in the palace garden for as long as anyone can remember. They are said to be older than the palace itself. They stood through the long years of The Repurrblic. They stood through the reign of first Caesars, until the time of the divine Augustpuss. With a crack and a puff of dust a branch snapped beneath my weight. From where I was clinging, it didn't look as if this cedar would stand my climbing for much longer.

Leaping carefully over to the opposite side of the tree, I got higher into the thick branches of the canopy. There was a shout from below. Dogren and Wulf had lost sight of me. But I knew better than to look down. For it is said that if a cat looks down whilst climbing a tree, the Goddess will turn his paws into stone and he will get himself stuck. It has happened to all of us.

Climbing higher, there was neither sight nor scent of the escaped Spraetorian. Then I heard a ringing and before I knew it, there were claws at my throat.

"Hold still. Don't try nothing or I'll skin you," said a voice. I held still.

"Who are you?" said the voice

"I'm Spartapuss," I replied, slipping slightly. "And would you mind if I moved from this branch because

I fear it could snap at any moment."

"Stay!" he ordered. "Who sent you?"

"The Purrmanians forced me to climb up here to try to get you to come down," I said.

"Well, you're welcome to try it, Ginger," he hissed.

"No thank you. I only climbed up because I didn't want to make them angry," I said.

"Well, you can tell them dammed Purrmanians that if they wants me, they'll 'ave to climb up 'ere themselves and get me," he said finally.

"I'd rather not tell them anything," I replied. Seeing that I was no assassin, he let me go.

MY CLIMBING PARTNER

When the Spraetorian stepped out from his hiding place, he told me that his name was Patchus. He was well named, for now I could see that he was all black save for a patch of white fur that covered his left eye. As I was finding out, there had always been fierce rivalry between the Spraetorian guards and the Purrmanian Bodyguards. Now this rivalry had turned to open hostility. The Purrmanians had heard rumours that assassins had been sent to kill the Emperor. The Bodyguards were sworn to protect the Emperor with their lives. Patchus had been stopped and caught in Purrmanian territory without papers. I was about to ask him what he was doing without papers but I thought better of it. I mouthed a silent thank you to Sussssh, the God of Tight

Lips, whom my friend Katrin had recommended to me back at Spatopia.

Patchus beckoned me forward.

"Follow me," he said, disappearing into a crack in the trunk. With a tight squeeze, a fit cat of medium build could just about wriggle inside. I am no longer a fit cat of medium build, for Bathhausia's Red Sausage dinners are exceedingly large, even after you scrape the sauce off. I got halfway though and found that I was stuck fast.

THE SAP SUCKERS

There is a certain shame that comes from being stuck up a tree that will bring a shudder to every cat that remembers their kittenhood. But this is nothing compared with the shame of being stuck in a tree – or to be more accurate, half way in and half way out. I cried out for help, but Patchus had gone. Looking up through the dark, I saw a point of light far above me. The ancient cedar was entirely hollow. I wondered what kind of bird might have hollowed out a great tree like this. Perhaps bee-eaters, sapsuckers or a family of greater spotted woodpeckers? I have never been fond of woodpeckers, for their beaks seem overlarge for their bodies. Bee-eaters are nasty flittery things but the thought of sapsuckers makes my stomach churn, as does the thought of any bird with a tongue.

In the darkness, I caught sight of a white circle, moving towards me. A terrible thought crossed my mind. Was it a white woodpecker or a bee-eater? Or was it a sapsucker protecting its nest? Had it now come to this? To be caught in the dark and pecked to death? Or to have the living sap sucked out of me?

Then Patchus appeared from the gloom. He was almost invisible, save for the white patch over his eye. Without a word he got hold the scruff of my neck and hauled me through the opening into the hollow centre of the tree.

I must confess that I have never had good eyesight. But as my eyes got used to the darkness, I began to make out a series of rungs, spiralling up the inside of the trunk. They were smooth to the touch and well worn but by the smell of them they had not been used for a long time. There was also a note of another smell that is not entirely tasteful to record.

"Who can have made this?" I asked. "It is surely not the work of woodpeckers!"

Patchus flicked his tail. "Peus knows, ginger! Spies most likely, or one of the cults. Follow me but go with care, I don't want you falling and giving us away to the Purrmanians."

He began to climb up. The steps had been carefully placed so that a fit cat could ascend at a great speed. Soon I was puffing and blowing. I called to Patchus to wait. But he was already far above me.

As I climbed the space got smaller as the trunk got thinner. Surely I was near the top of the tree now? At last the steps led out into a circular wooden platform with just enough space for us both to sit.

THE BOX IS OPENED

"Nice view of the city. You can see Paws Field from here," I said.

"Nice view of the palace, more like," said Patchus knowingly.

And he had a point. Whoever had built the platform must have been interested in the palace. From here you could make out the wall hangings in the Emperor's private apartments.

When I followed Patchus around the platform I found him crouched low to the ground, twitching like a soothsayer on his first sacrifice.

"What's the matter?" I whispered. A hiss of wind ruffled his fur as he spoke.

"In the legions we'll go against anything the barbarians can throw at us. We're trained for it. But there's bad magic here. Do you see the witches' writing?"

Set into the centre of the platform was a wooden box, covered in strange little pictures.

It was not the first time that I'd seen writing like this. It was Fleagyptian, the same as the writing on the coin that hung from my collar. Patchus and I had just one thought. What in the name of Mewpiter was inside the box?

Patchus' curiosity already had the better of him. He clawed at the box, trying to find a hidden clasp. There

32

was no hidden clasp. So he tore at the box with all his strength. But it would not yield. Exhausted, he kicked the lid in frustration.

Being a six claw, I have a strong grip. So I crouched, got a good hold and made ready to pull with all my strength. But there was no need. The moment I got my paws onto the box, the ancient fastenings popped open. Patchus let out a little mew of excitement. One good bit of witches' treasure was worth more than you'd get for your full sixteen years service in the Spraetorians!

"Give us first look, Ginger," he said with a hint of a growl in his voice.

"Help yourself!" I replied.

THE WITCHES' COLLAR
Patchus clawed the lid off and sniffed at the contents. Inside the box was set an old leather collar, with a large golden coin hanging at its centre. The coin was bigger than my own and was covered in more of what Patchus called 'witches' writing'. One of the symbols could have been a fish, another looked like a worm. I went to turn the coin over to examine the other side but Patchus held me back.

"Hold still Ginger. Maybe the witches put it here, for us to find." The wind blew again and shook the branches of the great cedar.

"I heard that the witches make you their slave once you wear their collar. you'll have to serve them for all your days and do their bidding, like a dog," he said.

It seemed to me that to be a dog was really not such a bad thing these days, compared to being a Gladiator or a sewer inspector. At least dogs enjoy their work. They are always wagging and slobbering all over the place with silly grins over their faces and eating out of our bowls when our backs are turned.

Perhaps Patchus agreed with this point of view because, even as he was warning me about the dangers of the witches, he was struggling to prise the coin from out of the collar. But it was impossible.

If I'd thought it was going to be dangerous in any way, I would have tried to stop him. But I knew that the writing on the collar was in the old Fleagyptian. "Don't worry. It's just like mine. Look," I said, unhooking my own coin from my collar. Edge to edge, the two coins looked as if they could have come from the same mint. The pale gold and the strange writing were identical. Except that Patchus' coin was larger and much grander than my own. The wind blew stronger again and I thought I heard shouts. Turning around, Patchus gave up trying to prise the coin out of its mounting and put the whole collar into a sack.

"Don't believe all of that nonsense about 'witches' collars'," I said.

But Patchus wasn't listening. His tail flicked. He'd caught the scent of something in the fields towards the palace.

"Spraetorians! A whole Scentury of the lads," he

said with satisfaction. "I knew they'd come."

And he pointed out Captain Matro, at the front of the column, 'for a change' as Patchus put it. Apparently the Spraetorians have their spies. As soon as the news of the fight had reached them, a rescue party had been sent out. Now they were marching in our direction, in a rather sloppy formation according to Patchus.

TUMBLE DOWN

On seeing the Spraetorians, Patchus shot down the ladder like a rat down a main drain. In my haste to follow him, I lost my footing and began to tumble head over tail. I tried sticking out a paw to slow my fall, but it was no use. I could only shout an apology as I fell past Patchus. Turning in mid air, I made ready for a heavy landing. With the crack of rotten wood, I crashed straight through a hidden door at the bottom of the tree trunk and rolled out into the sunlight, blinking like a kitten with its eyes newly-opened.

Hearing shouts, I sprung up and took off as quickly as my paws would carry me. With a terrible speed, my pursuers overtook me. Before I knew it, I was captured and blindfolded. Some wanted to take me back to the palace for a proper old-fashioned interrogation. Others said that time was short and so they must march on and interrogate me at the same time. Did I have any Purrmanian in me? I wasn't that big, but I certainly looked gingery enough. I told them I was a Kitton and known to their comrade Patchus. They tied up my front paws and got a rope on my collar. I said I was a freedcat and added that the rope was digging into my neck.

"Halt," said a voice too soft for barking orders.

As my blindfold was removed, a long-limbed figure padded forward. I noticed that his collar was of a regulation pattern but it had been remade out of the finest soft leather.

"I must offer my apologies Spartapuss," he purred. "I am Captain Matro. Firstly, thank you so much for coming to meet me at short notice. I'm very much looking forward to our meeting, but right now we're in a bit of a tight spot. Will you excuse me?"

He turned to speak to the big Scenturian, who was giving one of the recruits a dressing down for chasing butterflies.

"Could I have a word when you're finished?" purred the Captain.

"We're finished now, Sir!" bawled the Scenturian, giving the recruit a hard swipe and springing to attention.

"What do the spies report, Mewlius?" asked the Captain.

The recruit strained everything trying not to laugh. He had never heard his Scenturian's first name before.

"Yes Sir!" bawled the Scenturian uncomfortably. It was his Captain's way to be informal, but it was most embarrassing in front of the lads.

"We 'ave hout manoeuvred the Purrmanians, Sir! But Dogren will have our scent by now."

"Well I think we should get back to the barracks then, better make it at the double," said Matro.

"Yes Sir!" bawled the Scenturian.

But before the Scenturian could give the order to march, we heard a shout. "Halt! Friend or foe?"

"What's the watchword?" came the challenge.

"Neptuna," replied a familiar voice.

Patchus had escaped from the Purrmanians.

As a rule, the Spraetorians don't show their feelings. But it was obvious that their relief was great.

AT THE CAPTAIN'S TABLE

It was getting dark as we neared the palace and the guards saluted as we padded through the gates. Captain Matro stopped to talk to one of them. I started to thank Patchus for his help with the Purrmanians. He dismissed my thanks with a flick of the tail. Checking to see that I was not being overheard, I began to ask him whether he still had the 'witches' collar'. But before he could answer, the Scenturian gave the order to double back to barracks.

Now, I could think of nothing but dinner back at Bathhausia. I wondered if anything other than sausage would be on the menu. I went to take my leave of Captain Matro but he begged me to wait for just a moment. He said he had a proposal to discuss that would be very much in my interest. And as I was now at the palace, I may as well hear what he had to say. He was so polite that it seemed rude to refuse.

Captain Matro's office was not furnished in the plain style of the army. It was crammed with beautiful objects, taken from his victories all over the Empire. There were jewelled brushes in the Squeak style and all sorts of carvings in the style of conquered tribes of Purrmania. I even recognised a lucky rat's head carving from the land of the Kittons, where I come from. It had a squint and a nasty gap between its front teeth.

When he offered me a drink, I noticed that the Captain drank only the purest running water, from a silver fountain.

I said no to the drink but I complimented him on the lovely silverwork.

"That was a little present from Lady Mewlia herself," he sighed, adding "She will be sadly missed, Spartapuss."

The way he said it, I could almost believe that he meant it. Even though the Emperor's mother was one of least-loved cats in the entire Feline Empire.

"When you get down to it, the Imperial Family are just like you and me Spartapuss. They look after their own. And good servants deserve to be well rewarded for their loyalty." He made it sound perfect but I knew that was not always the way when you worked for the Imperials. When I worked for Clawdius before I was freed, I drank from an old wooden bowl. And when the woodworm ruined it, I'd had to work extra nights to buy a new one from him.

I settled on one of Matro's velvet cushions - I think it was in the shape of a Kati warrior, and listened.

"Look Spartapuss, I'll be brief for it has been a trying day for all of us. I hear that you have been freed by Clawdius but you haven't found a job yet. I also hear that you can read and write. So I want you to work for me, here at the palace as a scribe."

Fortune's wheel had turned and rolled my whole world over once again. This was a job interview. I was glad I was wearing my best collar.

"I expect you've got lots of questions," said Matro.

I had no clue what to say, except that it was a great surprise. For the Emperor Tiberius is not known to be a cat of letters and does not hold with the arts or literature. His main contribution to the arts had been to order the execution of two important poets and the drowning of an up-and-coming playwright. Similarities between the characters in their works and members of the Imperial Family had offended him.

"Would it be my duty to serve the Emperor personally?" I asked, trying not to sound too worried.

Matro smiled. "Of course, the Emperor and all members of the Imperial Family. They rarely bite! In fact it is a pleasure to serve them."

Before I could speak, he continued.

"Some would say that the honour of serving is payment enough. But your wages would be twenty silver coins per week as well as food and your own room here at the palace. The food here is excellent – there's roasted fish tonight."

A part of me wanted to jump for joy. It might have been the thought of something else for dinner other than sausages. Or it might have been the honour of being offered my first paid job. But I now did something very brave. I had little experience with money but I remembered that in business my old friend Russell had told me that it was never a good idea to agree to the first price that was mentioned.

"Captain Matro, I am overwhelmed by your most generous offer. But would it be possible to sleep on it and speak with you tomorrow?" I said.

Matro's tail gave the slightest of flicks but he smiled and said

"Of course, you must do just that. Goodbye until tomorrow then."

As I made my way out of the room he added,

"Spartapuss, make sure you give me your answer by midday tomorrow."

BACK TO SPATOPIA

I took my leave of Captain Matro thinking that I really do have fur for brains. I hoped that I hadn't displeased him. I needed advice so I headed for Spatopia. It is a long walk, but I went as usual by side streets and skirted gardens, careful to stay in neutral territory. As I approached the Spa gates, I wondered what sort of

40

a welcome I would get. I had no admission pass, for Clawdius had cancelled my membership. But there is a crack in the back wall near the Sacred Spring. I slipped through and padded directly to the kitchen where I knew I'd find Katrin. I was led on by the smell of roasting dormouse and the clatter of pewter bowls. Soon I was reclining in front of the kitchen fire as if I'd never been away, licking at one of Katrin's enormous dormouse kebabs. She was overjoyed to see me but I begged her not to make a fuss, for she does slobber rather. Under the circumstances I thought it best to keep my visit a secret. But she said that my friend Russell would be along presently.

"What troubles you Sparti dearest? You've hardly touched your lovely dormouse. Was there too much salt on the tail?" she asked. Actually I thought I was doing rather well, the kebab was never ending and surely too wide to be a dormouse.

"I have some news," I said, as I toyed with my food.

"I was going to wait until Russell arrives. But I must tell you now. I have been offered a job at the palace. It's a great opportunity. I am to be a scribe for the Imperial Family. I may even be asked write down the words of the Emperor Tiberius himself."

"Mother of Klaws! No wonder you've lost your appetite," cried Katrin.

She sniffed the air, stepped closer and lowered her voice.

"Sparti, I know that you are a freedcat now, but the

palace is a dangerous place. The Emperor grows old and he has not officially picked an heir. The palace is full of plots, like a Squeak tragedy."

"But I have to work somewhere," I said.

"Please Sparti, can't you come back?" she asked.

That was the problem. I was free but without a patron. I had no money. I had little choice but to accept Captain Matro's job. My thoughts were interrupted by the flap of wings and a crash. Evidently my friend Russell had not made much progress on his landings. Katrin explained the situation.

"Clawdius would never agree to your return," said Russell in his deep voice.

"He is too stubborn. And he thinks that you are a bad pawtent."

"He is right about something then," hissed another voice, as bitter as a lemon grove in the winter.

"And I wonder what he'll think about his ex-slave breaking in here in the middle of the night and conspiring with his servants?" spat Mogullania.

A BITTER SPITTER

It was the first time that I'd spoken to Clawdius' new wife, but the reputation that went before her was not pleasant. She was said to be more of a spitter than a circler. It is whispered that Clawdius' grandmother Mewlia forced him into marrying Mogullania as a punishment. Yet it was Mogullania who always wore a weary expression whenever she was with her husband, as if she had lost a rabbit and found a mouse.

She turned on me.

"You! You are not allowed in here. Get out now or I shall call the guards and have you put out," she hissed.

I wanted to explain myself but I could not find the words. Katrin tried for me.

"If Master Clawdius would only speak with Spartapuss I'm sure…" she began. But it was hopeless. Mogullania was the hardest heart from a litter of stones.

She turned on me again.

"You think that if you see Clawdius and give him some excuses then all will be right again. But it will never be all right. You humiliated him with your ridiculous behaviour at the Arena."

"That wasn't Spartapuss' fault," said Katrin.

"That is not how Clawdius sees it," spat Mogullania.

"Why don't we ask him?" said Russell.

CLAWDIUS' JUDGEMENT

Clawdius padded into the kitchen, dragging his bad leg behind him as usual. His limp was worse than I remembered. He walked with a peculiar little roll, as if his hind legs had their own mind and refused to march in step with his front legs.

Mogullania could not bear the way everyone stared at him and she now insisted that the two of them were carried everywhere in a cushioned chair. If anything, this was making the problem worse as he needed more exercise.

"Can someone tell me what this is this about?" asked Clawdius, without stumbling over his words this time.

This was my chance to say my piece. But it was as if some other cat had got my tongue. In the end it was Russell who spoke for me.

"Spartapuss has come to ask for his old job back. He would like to come back..."

"And ruin you again," interrupted Mogullania.

Then I heard myself saying:

"Clawdius, I am sorry if I have offended you in any way. As you know, I was a loyal servant to you for many years and I would like to serve you again, as a freedcat."

His expression seemed to soften. I was sure that he too was sorry. But then he backed away.

"M-Mogullania runs everything now," he said.

"Don't worry," I said. "Captain Matro has offered me a job at the palace."

Mogullania coughed as if she was choking on a fur ball. Katrin glanced at Russell knowingly. Then Mogullania recovered herself.

"Clawdius, how long will you stand here, waiting on your own slaves?" she hissed.

Clawdius did not reply, he turned and headed for the door in his rolling walk. My audience was over. Mogullania had got what she wanted, but she didn't seem much happier for it. And she had a parting shot.

"Work hard at the palace Spartapuss. And don't forget your Gladiator's trident, for it is a nest of vipers."

"She speaks the truth there," said Russell, when he was sure she was out of earshot. He had to wait a long time, for Mogullania has big ears.

APURILIS XIII

April 13th

Two Scrolls for the Scribe

AND SO HERE I SIT in my scribing room, behind my new scribing desk, sitting on one of my comfortable cushions. A Spraetorian brought it in, with the compliments of Captain Matro. In front of me are two scrolls and a pot of ink. One scroll is very long and of the finest quality paper. I shall need it in my official work as an Imperial scribe. The other scroll is for this – my diary. I shall continue writing it now, because Captain Matro says that one can't get enough scribing practice.

APURILIS XIV

April 14th

A Room with a View

MY ROOM AT THE PALACE is nice and warm. I have a beautiful view of the palace gardens. There is not much to report. I am not wanted for scribing today.

APURILIS XV

April 15th

A Room with No View

TODAY THE SPRAETORIAN GUARDS came in and installed my new shutters. These are the latest thing in security, offering me great protection. The guards who installed them did not say who I am to be protected against but we thought that it was probably to guard against spies. But also the tree opposite has a family of woodpeckers in it and they have been known to get aggressive in the spring. Captain Matro has still not called on me to do any scribing. There is nothing to do but sharpen my nib and have a little sleep at my cushion by the window.

APURILIS XVI

April 16th

Not Today, Thank You!

MY NIB IS SHARP and my claws are sharper. I haven't been out of the palace all week. This morning I went to Captain Matro's office to ask if I was needed. I found the office empty but there was a familiar musky smell about the place. Outside in the corridor I met a group of cleaners. They were so busy talking and laughing that they didn't see me coming. I startled one of them and she leapt up, shouting for the guards, who came. By a lucky spin from Fortune's wheel, one of the Spraetorians recognised me. He said that he was sorry to hear that no one had any call for scribing but, no, he didn't think that he or the other guards needed any scribing today. He said that he and the lads prefer fighting to writing, which I suppose is a passable joke, for a soldier. He insisted on escorting me back to my room. On the way back, I discovered the cause of his good humour. The Purrmanian Bodyguards have all gone to the island of Capri, where the Emperor is at his holiday villa. This has left the Spraetorian guard with the run of the palace.

APURILIS XVII

April 17th

A Boat Dream

PERHAPS IT IS SOMETHING in the atmosphere here in the palace, or perhaps last night's roasted cod was rotten. But on falling asleep, I had a dream so vivid that I had all four paws in it as they say. I was running up a cliff path, towards a magnificent villa. The path was steep and the dark sea was crashing somewhere below. At least I think it was crashing, for I heard no sounds throughout the whole dream. When I looked down at the rocks and foam, I almost lost my balance. Then everything stopped and I found myself in a sickroom, judging by the smell of the herbs and grasses. Slowly, I approached the bed. But I can remember no more.

I am not superstitious by nature and I get away with making only those sacrifices that are called for by law. But this dream has unnerved me. Is it a bad pawtent? Now I would call for a dream interpreter but, sadly, they were banned by the Emperor Tiberius after they kept predicting deaths in the Imperial Family and getting their dates wrong.

APURILIS XVIII

April 18th

Crow at the Shutters

NOTHING COULD HAVE PREPARED ME for what has happened this week. I must have offended all the gods of Mount Olympuss. I used to think that most of them were for me, except perhaps Backus, the God of Long Odds. But now I am sure they have all been playing with me like a caught mouse.

I shall take up the story from last night, when I went to bed in a state of dread, hoping that I would not be troubled by more dreams. I had deliberately stuck to plain dishes for dinner, as I have a theory about the cooks here. The special ingredient that they put into their mouse mousse is not what they say it is. I had only just curled up on my cushion when I heard a tapping at the window. I took it for the wind at my shutters, ignored it and willed myself back to sleep. But it did not go away. The tap became a knocking. I crept silently to the window. The Spraetorians had locked down my shutters as usual but I could just get a view through the slats.

"Well met my friend Spartapuss," said Russell. "I am come to you with an important message."

"From Clawdius?" I asked eagerly.

"Not from Clawdius," he replied. "I have been sent by the sister of Cleocatra the cleaner," he cleared his throat slightly before saying the name.

"Cleocatra? What in Peus' name can she want?" I sighed. There was to be no making up with Clawdius. No return to Spatopia. Mogullania's heart was set like concrete, against my return.

"Spartapuss," said Russell seriously, "do you understand me? Cleocatra's SISTER sent me."

Then I understood. Cleocatra's sister Tefnut is what some would call a mystic. I owe her a great debt, for she taught me the ancient art of Ring Raking, which I used to defend myself at the Games of Purrcury. I have not seen her since.

"What was her message?" I asked.

"She told me to look carefully to see whether or not you were wearing the golden coin she gave you on your collar. But I can't see. If you are not wearing it, do not put it on. But if you are wearing it, please take it off now."

For a bird to come to your window at night and ask you to take your collar off would strike most Romans as a very unusual request. But knowing that the Fleagyptians have strange customs, and remembering how stubborn my friend could be, I decided that there could be no harm in going along with it. Knowing Tefnut, it was probably some strange ritual from out of the East.

"All right," I said, "I'll take it off now."

TIGHT FIT

As I slipped a paw under my collar it seemed to fit me a little tighter than usual. Perhaps all that rich food from the Imperial kitchens had fattened up my neck. They serve us rich pickings, left over from the Imperial banquets. I tried to slip it off my neck, but the wretched thing would not budge. It really was tighter. Digging into the old leather with my claws, I got a good grip and pulled. But it was no use, it was stuck fast. The more I pulled, the tighter it became. I started to panic, rolling round the floor as I twisted to prise the wretched thing from my neck. But the harder I pulled, the tighter it became. Soon I started to choke as if on a fur ball.

"Stop!" shouted Russell. "You cannot get it off like that,"

"I'll cut it off!" I cried, searching for a blade that would hack through tough leather.

"It is no use tearing the palace apart my friend," said Russell. "The Emperor banned anything with a sharp edge from the servants' rooms many years ago, after that protester from Cathens got into his bedroom."

Exhausted, I rolled onto my back and caught my breath.

"And you will need more than a knife get that collar off. It is just as she foretold," he added.

"Really?" I replied, unhappy to learn that I'd been the subject of any "foretelling". Whenever foretelling happens, it means ill fortune for someone.

Then I remembered Patchus' words in the Cedar tree

when he had found his gold coin. A 'witches' collar' he had called it. Once you wear it, you have to do their bidding like a dog. I cursed myself for my stupidity! Why had I ever put the coin onto the collar in the first place? If it was dangerous, why had Tefnut given it to me? I would find out soon enough, for Russell had one more message to deliver. He told me to be at the cave of the Moracle at sunrise next morning.

TO THE CAVE OF THE MORACLE

It is a long way to the Moracle's cave. I have not measured the distance on a map, but it is currently outside the perimeter of the hated Chariot Charge (although it is said that the tax collectors have asked the Senate to expand the Charge zone as far as the city limits). My journey would have been easier if the shutters in my room were not locked. I had to creep downstairs and through the kitchen without attracting the attention of the guards. As Fortune spun it, the Spraetorian guarding the gate was Patchus, who I'd met in the cedar tree. I gave him the excuse that I had been summoned for some important midnight scribing by the Imperial Family. He accepted this story without question.

"Fortune marches with you Ginger," he said.

"Come Patchus. I'll bet you're the richest Spraetorian in the palace yourself. A coin like the one on that collar you found in the tree must be worth ten years' pay. But a word of advice if I may be allowed — on no account put it on."

Patchus let out a hiss.

"It's gone," he said. "The Purrmanians took it."

It pained Patchus more than any of his old wounds to think of the prize he'd lost. He'd been planning to buy himself out of the army with the money from the Fleagyptian coin. He wanted to set himself up in a shop selling roasted dormouse to the army. But Rome needs another cheap dormouse shop like it needs a hole in the sewer. And as for the collar that came with the coin, he has no clue how lucky he is that he never put it on.

The night grew old as I picked my way through the narrow streets away from the palace. The night traders were still at their stalls and the moon was high in the sky. We Romans are a plain lot. We are very straightforward creatures, who like the rule of law and our gods are the same: brutal at times, but mostly predictable.

The Fleagyptians however, are mysterious creatures. They like to do everything in secret. So it is strange to think that every Roman, even the youngest kitten, knows the whereabouts of the most powerful and ancient Fleagyptian temple in the city. The way to the Moracle's cave is not difficult or secret because we Romans like that sort of thing to be clearly marked on our tourist maps.

Fortune-telling was also banned by the Emperor Tiberius when he grew weary about the predictions of his own death. In an angry fit one night, he exiled all fortune-tellers beyond the city walls saying, "You rats didn't predict that, did you?"

It is a matter of fact that many of the fortune-tellers crept straight back in that same night and started up their businesses again in the safer line of soothsaying. As far as I can tell, this is fortune-telling without the star charts. And it has a better line in souvenirs. But the Moracle was never subject to the Emperor's ban on fortune-telling because the Moracle's cave is outside the city walls. It is perched up in the dry hills, near to the place where the ancients used to bury their dead. It is considered a pretty spot to view the city and on festivals and feast days the cream of Roman society can be seen padding up the winding path in order to get their fortunes read. They sniff their way past the lemon groves and puff as they climb the rocky path up the marble steps, and through the White Arch to the temple. But they will get no further than the yard outside the Moracle's cave, where the Soothsayers have set up their stalls. the Moracle is very particular about who she will see. Not even Emperors are guaranteed a reading. If the Moracle has something to tell you, you are summoned to the inner temple to hear it.

And so it was that I found myself climbing the steps and padding under the White Arch to the yard where the soothsayers were getting ready for the new day's tourists. The most popular souvenir is a model of the White Arch with the inscription 'I visited the Moracle but all I got was this White Arch'.

The souvenirs were all marked with the symbol of the Moracle: a great white snake coiled in a circle - swallowing its own tail in a rather disgusting manner. I searched the stalls for Tefnut but there was no sign.

Then a voice said:

"Come and look! The most potent charm you can buy. The Great Snake that eats his own tail. He forms a circle that symbolises the Wheel of Time. The Wheel that turns forever as each of us dies and is reborn."

"No charms thank you," I said.

You had to be firm with these soothsayers, they simply would not give up until you bought a guided tour, and a model arch and a souvenir drinking bowl and all.

"Come!" said the soothsayer. "Come on my tour and see wonders. Come and see the Wheel turn!" I was not at all tempted by her offer. She reeked of incense, for one thing. And she would not look me in the eye.

"The Wheel doesn't look like it would turn very well," I observed, trying to put her off. "The Snake God's head is sticking up like a nail. There'd be a nasty bump whenever Time rolls over him. I expect he gets terrible headaches."

But the soothsayer was used to dealing with ignorant tourists. She ignored the question and beckoned me onwards with all the skill of a trained guide.

"Step with me now under the Scared Arch and the mysteries of the temple shall be revealed."

I was about to tell her "No!" again when I smelt

something familiar about her. There was also something about her voice, underneath the heavy Fleagyptian accent. At last I got a look at her eyes. They were big green eyes that shone like lamps. I drew closer.

"Tefnut?" I asked in a whisper.

"Yes," she replied quietly, before continuing in a loud voice:

"Step under the White Arch. Your tour of the Cave of the Moracle begins by the waterfall."

TOURIST TRAP

I had first met Tefnut at Gladiator training school, where she'd given me private lessons in an ancient Fleagyptian self defence technique. I had not seen her since the night before the Games. I'd had no chance to thank her for her teaching, which had saved my life that day. She'd also given me the coin that was attached to my collar. Now she had summoned me. Surely, she'd know how to get the wretched collar off.

In my excitement to follow my old tutor, I almost tripped over a loose paving stone. This could have been a disastrous way of attracting unwanted attention, as there are so many lawyers in the city these days.

As we entered the temple, I noticed that the underside of the arch was covered in 'witches' writing' as Patchus would call it. The roof of the chamber was lit by the flicker of many lights.

"The Eyes of the Gods," said Tefnut the guide, with

a sweeping gesture.

"It's just a lot of old lamps, they've got them on hidden shelves up there," said a voice from another tour group. Voices carried far inside the Cave of the Moracle.

The cave itself was like a gaping mouth in the hillside, chiselled out of the black rock with delicate blows and polished like a beach pebble. Carved into the roof was the symbol of the Snake God. There was something quite disturbing about the Great Snake eating itself. It was like dogs chasing their own tails, but taken one revolting step further.

I had many questions for Tefnut, but we were not alone. The hall was packed with tourists, for the sunrise tour was in fashion at the moment.

"Come!" said Tefnut with another theatrical gesture.

She stopped near the back of the cave by a waterfall that crashed down the rock with great force. The plumbing was most impressive. Many lead pipes just a few whiskers thick spilled the water into a great marble basin. The basin was decorated with carvings of all manner of sea creatures. The swordfish and the giant clam were accurate but the dolphin might have been better carved. There was some poor chisel work around its nose.

"Behold the Sacred Pool!" said Tefnut. Still playing the guide, she turned around to face me, turning her back to the waterfall. Always get the tourist looking at you as well as the landmark! Then she spoke as if from memory:

"This historic fountain was a gift from the God Augustpuss, carved by the master Stone Carver, Marbipuss when Fluffius and Nipro were consuls, in the year of..."

The other tourists were busy craning their necks at the great white snake in the roof. Tefnut caught my eye.

"Do not think about what to do next, just follow me," she said. Then to my amazement she threw herself backwards and vanished into the heart of the waterfall.

TREAD WATER

I stared into the falls. There was no sign of Tefnut, not even a bubble. Gazing into the flood I could understand why the barbarians cannot stand running water. I myself used to hate it. But I soon became accustomed to it when I was brought to Rome from my home in the land of the Kittons, where it is said that the tribes never wash. We Romans love our baths of course, but we are not a nation of swimmers. Tefnut's teachings had saved me in the Arena. I had seen her do many impossible things. Perhaps the waterfall was an illusion set there to impress the tourists. Convinced that she would never willingly put me into peril I decided that I had to follow.

I leapt up onto the rim of the marble basin. I could feel the mist rising from the falls now.

The water was icy, springing straight from the veins of the mountain. Deciding that a backwards somersault was beyond my skill, I decided to go gently. Mouthing a silent prayer to Neptuna, God of the Sea, I counted to three and flung myself nose first into the pool. I waited for Tefnut's magic to work. But there was no magic. I sunk like a stone in the dark water. I tried to kick for the surface but the cold had turned my legs to concrete. Caught by the currents, I stuck out a paw and held on to the first thing I could. It was the base of a statue. Clawing myself up, I somehow managed to make the surface. Now I found myself half way down the pool, clinging to the back of a statue of a giant clam. The falls were closer now and in the crash of the water I thought I heard cries. Lost souls in the pool or the spirit of Neptuna calling through the mists?

"Spartapuss!" they seemed to call.

But I shut my ears to their cries. For I have heard tales of the Siamese sailors, lured onto the rocks by haunting calls of beautiful sea spirits.

"Over here!" a faint voice was calling. Hovering in the middle of the pool, near the blunt-nosed dolphin, stood Tefnut. I have seen many of her magic tricks before, but even I was amazed to see her actually walking on water.

"Help!" I cried. "Quickly! Use your magic!"

"Use your eyes!" she replied.

Set a whisker's length under the surface were a series of stepping-stones. They had been carved out of black marble, making them invisible unless you knew exactly where to look. They formed a path that led statue by statue towards the crashing waterfall. I wasted no time in picking my way through towards the dolphin where Tefnut had been standing. From here I could see how the water crashed down over the lip of the rock. I could even see through the falls themselves. Carved under the arch, where no one would see it, was more 'witches' writing', and the Snake that eats itself again. But in the middle of the circle - like the hub of a great wheel, was a picture of another animal. I couldn't quite make it out.

"Hurry," called Tefnut.

In a few short bounds I passed through the curtain of falling water into a dry cave behind.

BEHIND THE CURTAIN

Safe on a rock, I cleaned up as best as I could and picked some pondweed out of my ruff. I wondered if Tefnut would be angry.

"A fine fish you make! With that wet fur you look half your size," she laughed. Naturally, she had remained bone dry.

"As you have guessed, this is the entrance to the Cave of the Moracle," she continued. "This is the real one, the other one is for the tourists. It is a rare honour to be granted an audience. The Moracle usually only speaks to Emperors and kings."

"Are you sure the Moracle wants to see me?" I asked. "Perhaps there's been some misunderstanding. Only I seem to have got this collar stuck around my neck and now I can't get it off. I was hoping..."

"You were hoping that I could get if off for you. Indeed. That collar of yours has got us into a lot of trouble. I fear that you'll need to wear it for a while yet. Have you perhaps come across another one like it, by any chance?" asked Tefnut as she flicked her tail and sat waiting for my answer.

I explained about the Purrmanian guards and Patchus, the hollow cedar tree and the ancient box.

"And this Patchus, did he put the other collar on?" asked Tefnut.

"No - he said it was dangerous. He was going to prise the coin out and melt it down."

Tefnut's tail flicked once again but she said nothing.

"Patchus said it was a 'witches' collar'," I began.

"Did he?" said Tefnut. "And what do you think? Has anything unusual happened? Did he get the coin out and melt it down?"

"No. He could not get it off. His collar was taken by the Purrmanian Bodyguards."

Tefnut nodded.

"Is mine a 'witches' collar' too? I mean, I didn't do anything. I only put the gold coin you gave me onto my collar because I wanted to make a good impression at the palace. I never bought any charms or anything. But ever since I climbed the tree, I've not been able to get the collar off."

Tefnut said nothing.

"I should never have opened that box, only Patchus

had been so kind in helping to get me away from the Purrmanians. It's my own fault. I should never…"

"Enough!" said Tefnut. "Now hear my words Spartapuss, and really listen this time, for this is a serious matter."

She stopped and flicked her tail. There was something unusual about her movements. She circled around, uneasily. When she settled, her green eyes wandered from the roof to the cave floor. I had never seen her behave like this before. She almost seemed embarrassed. Finally, she announced:

"In short, the two collars, yours and the one that you and Patchus found up the cedar tree, have become joined. There is an old saying that explains it."

'Wherever you go, I will be,
Whatever you see, I can see,
Whenever I call, you must answer,
Until I'm undone, you will never be free.'

On finishing the verse, she sat down on a rock, looking as if there was nothing more to be said.

As far as I was concerned, the saying didn't explain anything.

"And so now I must do the witches' bidding, like a dog!" I howled.

"Spartapuss, you must forget all of these kittens' tales about witches and listen."

"But how can I get it off!" I cried. I started to

scratch and claw at the collar. Just as before, I felt it tighten around my neck and begin to draw the breath out of me.

"Cease!" hissed Tefnut, drawing herself up to her full height. Her green eyes flashed at me.

"You cannot get it off. It has become joined to the other collar. Someone is wearing the other one now. Unless they take theirs off, nothing can remove yours."

"Can't you use some magic to get it off?" I begged.

"You have not been listening. Nothing can get it off."

That didn't sound good.

"But..." I began.

"If I were to chop of your head, it would cling to the bloody stump of your neck," she added.

I began to howl.

"Spartapuss, there is little time. You must be calm. We cannot have you running about like a puppy off its lead. Remember that whoever has the other collar can see whatever you see. If they know how it works."

"Can they hear us, what we're saying now. I mean..."

"No – they cannot hear words. The old ones who made it did not speak in words but in pictures, like these."

She pointed at the witches' writing on the wall of the cave.

"The collar lets you see through another's eyes, if you know how."

"And the Moracle?" I asked. "What has the Moracle to do with all of this?"

Tefnut arched her back and then circled again. It was a while before she replied.

"That, I do not know. In a moment the sun will have risen and you will be summoned. When you enter the chamber, remember the Moracle's words exactly. Like all oracles, she speaks in riddles. When you are in the cave, you will see things that seem strange. But I suppose you are expecting that already."

I walked towards a low door at the back of the cave. On it was another picture of the white snake swallowing its own tail. A thought occurred to me.

"Tefnut," I asked. "Is there anything else that you might want to tell me. I mean, is the Moracle guarded?"

She had an annoying habit of laughing when I was at my most serious.

"Yes - of course it is guarded. But you will not be in danger from the Observer, you are an invited guest."

I didn't look convinced but Tefnut smiled.

"Go now, for the sun is almost risen. You are expected. I will be here when you return."

She motioned towards the door at the back of the cave. As I approached, I could see a picture in the centre of the snake inscription. It was faded and I couldn't work out quite what it was. There was an unusual smell to the place, which was masked by burning incense. The door swung slowly open to reveal a chamber lit by bright sunlight. The walls were covered in more drawings of the Great Snake. I trod on something. It was transparent and flaky to the touch. A tiny beam of cold light streamed in from a shaft in the roof. I could make out more of the transparent stuff, littering the floor in piles. My first thought was rituals – oracles loved them. I hoped that this was not some unpleasant ritual that Tefnut had neglected to tell me about.

What little light there was fell in a thin shaft onto the marble altar where a box had been placed. On closer inspection, the box was made of a kind of gold mesh. It had a triangular door in its side. In the middle of the box was what looked like a tiny cartwheel, only it was hollow and free spinning, like a water wheel. It was supported on both sides by tiny carved serpents. Peus alone knows what the purpose of this machine could be, but it hadn't been placed there by accident! Carved onto the sides of the wheel was my old friend, the snake that eats itself.

THIS IS THE WAY, STEP INSIDE

A noise from faraway drew my attention from the altar. I wondered where the Moracle would appear from. Every oracle and soothsayer that I have heard of has gone in for a dramatic entrance. I circled uneasily. Perhaps the Moracle would sliver down from on high. Maybe she'd be carried in on a chair by assistants. I have a strong dislike of assistants. They have such a haughty attitude. I suppose they are trained for it. If only the Moracle would get on with it, for I couldn't stand much more waiting!

Gazing up at the light, I wondered if the shaft led all the way up to the summit of the mountain. If so, it must have taken an age to cut. Such a work would be too expensive to undertake these days because of the high costs of the labour. It is almost impossible to find a skilled stone carver to be had in the city. Certainly the ancients who built this temple went in for grand designs that would put us to shame. Clawdius used to say that they knew how to get the best out of their workers in those days, when the whip and the muzzle were your work mates. Not like it is now with the guilds of construction workers and their regulations. Whilst I was thinking such thoughts I had not noticed that the triangular door at the side of the box had swung wide open. Out of the box came a mouse.

Tefnut had told me to prepare for strange sights but this was most unexpected. I now found myself talking to a mouse, and a tiny white one at that.

"Hello," I said. "I'm Spartapuss. I'm here to see the Moracle. Do you think you could let them know I'm here? It's all right, I've been summoned."

The little white mouse laughed at my uneasy introduction. Suddenly I realised that she was the Moracle. How embarrassing! I hoped I hadn't offended her.

"Many apologies, oh wise Moracle," I began, not knowing how to address a Moracle. It was at times like this that I wished I'd studied Squeak or

66

Fleagyptian but I only know Catin and the language from my homeland

"I hope I didn't offend you," I said. "Only I was expecting something else,"

The Moracle laughed again.

"You were expecting a lot of haughty assistants followed by a great fat snake, stuffing its tail into its great white jaws," thought the Moracle. And as she thought, I could hear her inside my head. Although she spoke no words, I could understand her just the same.

"You read my mind!" I said in wonder.

"I didn't have to," thought the Moracle. "The great fat snake is what they all expect. Why do you think we have gone to the trouble of painting pictures of it all over the place?"

"Oh wise Moracle," I said formally. "Why have you summoned me here? Surely there has been some mistake. I am but a humble scribe, recently a freedcat."

"You know why you are here," thought the Moracle.

"You ran up a tree and opened a box
And in it you found a collar long lost…"

Tefnut was right, it was going to be a lot of riddles. And it was not the best riddling I had heard, either.

"Thank you for your advice, great Moracle," I said, at the same time realising that 'great' wasn't the best way to describe a mouse. I didn't want her to take offence.

"And now that I have heard your prophecy, may I please be excused, for there is much scribing to do this week at the Imperial Palace."

The Moracle held me in her gaze.

"Stay, freed-cat. You have not had my prophecy yet. You will know it, when you have heard it," thought the Moracle.

"Where have I heard that before?" I thought to myself.

She began to chew upon some biscuits that covered the floor of the house. Then she jumped into the wheel and began to run and run. The wheel turned but the Moracle, now running hard remained still. Then the lights went out and I began to dream. Only it was as if someone had taken a torch and lit up my usual dreams so that I could see into every corner. Even the sun of my dreams shone brighter than in life!

Now I cannot record here exactly what I dreamed, for you cannot properly describe a dream in words. We dream in pictures, like the ancient Fleagyptians used to write in pictures. And as the great Cato says, '...each cat's dream is for themselves alone'. But I shall try to set it down here in words anyway, for it would be a poor scribe if I gave up at my first challenge. As for the colours and the scents and the feelings, you will have to fill all of them in for yourself.

THE WITNESS

I was in a boat, looking out over waters dark as squid ink as we neared an island. And as I looked out, I knew it was a dream and I knew that I had dreamed it before. Only this time I was dreaming with my eyes open. I knew it was the island of Capri. I knew that the piles of wood on the shore were fires of mourning. They had not been lit but the scented wood had been freshly cut. Then I was running along a rock path that rose up the cliff-side towards the Emperor's private villa. I was in a hurry, the path was steep and the sharp stones cut my pads. Below me, the sea toyed with a stray barrel, dragging it over submerged rocks as sharp as eagle's beaks. The waves crashed. Or at least, they should have crashed. I felt them rumble but I realised that I could hear no sound in this dream. Turning a corner, I slipped and broke a claw on the sharp rock. I felt a pain like a needle and examined my paw. The pads were pale pink and soft. They had never scrubbed scum off a plunge pool. It took me a moment to work out what was wrong. There were only five claws on the each of my front paws, and I have six. I was not myself. I was seeing the world through another's eyes. I got up and ran on along the path.

Whoever I was in this dream had an important appointment to keep. Without asking, the answers revealed themselves. My appointment was with the Emperor himself. He was near to death and I had to reach him before death took him. And there was something else. The thought of his death gave me great pleasure.

At last I felt the marble steps under my pads as I made my way to the gates. The villa was guarded by the Imperial Bodyguards. The Purrmanians saluted as I passed but avoided my eyes. Was I too late? The court-yard was packed with senators and their servants, all waiting for news. The atmosphere was frantic. I heard no sound but again, my questions were answered. I knew what they were saying. Would the Emperor wake again from his sleep? Who had he named as his heir to rule Rome after him?

Two Squeak doctors waited outside the Emperor's sickroom. He had sent to the farthest reaches of his Empire for a cure. The doctors looked grave and concerned and for a good reason. Old Tiberius had dug his claws into what life he had left. His will left instructions that if he died unexpectedly his doctors were to follow him into the next world.

At my command, they opened the panelled door and I entered the sickroom. It was hung with rich silks and littered with golden bowls, each one containing a different medicine. The scent of saffron covered another smell - rotten and overpowering. I closed the door and dismissed the slaves. Slowly, I approached the bed. Tiberius lay on a great pile of cushions, not moving a whisker. I stalked towards him. The famous head that was carved on hundreds of statues all over Rome, was lolling.

The ruler of the world had very common markings. He looked as if someone had started making a cheap mosaic on his face, from black and white tiles, but had stopped for lunch and left the work unfinished. I drew closer and lifted up an ear. It was torn from his many campaigns against the tribes of Purrmania. Drawing my mouth close to his leathery ear, I shouted: "Tiberius! Tiberius!" There was no movement.

Just to check, I took hold of a whisker and pulled hard. But the ruler of the known world lay still as set concrete.

Delighted, I grabbed the golden claw from his cold grasp. It was the Imperial Seal, the symbol of the empire I would inherit. Waving the claw aloft, I rushed out of the door, down the corridor and into the courtyard to address the crowd.

I could not hear my words or their replies but I knew what I was saying. Their Emperor was dead – and he had named me as his heir. They swam around me like little minnows in a jar, all wanting to offer their congratulations to their new Emperor.

Then I saw the two doctors running towards me. The Purrmanians held them back. I knew exactly what they were shouting. The Emperor Tiberius was not dead. He had just called for his cod supper and a bowl of milk. And he wanted his Golden Claw back – whoever had stolen it was to be thrown from the cliff. The Purrmanian guards stood claws out at the ready. What was the meaning of this? I cried, calling for the guards – who were standing around looking sheepish. A Scenturian led me away from the crowd and together we ran back to the sickroom. We spoke. When our conversation was over, I was pleased. The army always knew what to do. The Scenturian took two guards with him and went back into the Emperor's sickroom. I waited outside that door for five minutes, filing my claws. And when they all came out puffing, as if they'd just left the gymnasium, I knew that the Emperor of the known world was dead. They gave me the Golden Claw again. Soon, I would address the crowd. On a whim, I walked over to a looking glass and held the claw up high, practising my expressions. Then I noticed the collar around my neck. From it hung a large gold coin. It was covered in witches' writing. And as I put my paw to my collar, the vision ended.

GONE GONE GONE

The first thing I was aware of was the collar, tight around my neck. Light streamed into the cave from a shaft in the ceiling. It was ordinary daylight and not the weird light of the vision. The Moracle was off her wheel - and it spun slowly to a halt. She was watching me with an interested eye.

"Yes, it is over, and no you cannot take it off. Not till his own collar is off," thought the Moracle in answer to my unspoken questions.

"Remember what you saw today. For once, you

will be the spinner and Rome's fortune will depend on your choice." With those words, the Moracle, looking drained from her effort on the wheel, turned to go back into her house.

I heard shouts echoing from the heart of the mountain. Someone had raised the alarm.

"Come back!" I pleaded. "I don't understand. Does it mean that the Emperor is dead?"

The Moracle turned to answer me, but her thoughts were disturbed by a crash. The wooden doors on both sides swung open and a company of Spraetorian guards burst into the chamber. Before I could get another word out, two of them had scooped up the Moracle, house and all, and loaded her onto a cart. The Scenturian, a wiry looking tabby, was shouting at parade ground volume. He didn't seem to have noticed me. Another two Spraetorians were tearing at a beautiful wall hanging. They pulled and pulled but they could not get it off the wall. Exhausted, they stopped clawing at it and looked at their captain.

"By 'Ercatules' claws, ain't any of you mice ever taken down an 'anging in your grandmuvver's 'ouse before? Mogrippus – get a grip of it for Peus' sake!" bawled the Scenturian.

Then he noticed me.

"What's your name and why are you still 'ere?" he asked. And before I could answer, he added:

"Are you a priest?"

"No, I'm a scribe," I replied. "At the Imperial Palace,"

I added, hoping that it might count for something.

"My name is Spartapuss. I was here for a reading," I went on. "They told me to wait."

Behind him there was a crash as the wall hanging finally came quietly.

"It's not closing time is it? I hope the gift stalls haven't shut," I said.

"What? 'Aven't you 'eard?" growled the Scenturian. "The Emperor's dead. It's ten days of mourning and all festivities cancelled as usual. Poor old Tibbles! He was an awful 'ard case, but he was loved by the legions." There was almost a tear in his eye as he said this.

"That is ill news," I said sympathetically.

"All officials 'ave been recalled to Rome," he said matter-of-factly, "So You'd better get a move on."

I thanked him and stalked off as fast as I could without attracting any more attention.

THE OBSERVER

The number three is said by the Kittons to be magical and lucky. Yet I must confess that it has never brought me good fortune. So I was dismayed to find three paths leading from the Moracle's cave. Making a fast choice, I picked the one that the guards had taken when they ended my reading with the Moracle. The path led upwards. As I walked, I tried to reason. The Emperor was dead, murdered perhaps, as my vision had foretold. And now the Spraetorians had taken the Moracle, house and all – and she hadn't foretold that, had she?

74

Where in Peus' name was Tefnut when I needed her? I decided that the only thing to do was to get back to the palace before Captain Matro noticed that I was missing. The path wasn't helping, it had started out heading upwards but now it was twisting down again. I was thinking about turning back when the rock of the tunnel gave way to chill air. A cold wind ruffled my coat. I had reached the end of the road and now I looked out over a long drop. I was the sole visitor to this town in the centre of the mountain. I had come to the place where the ancients used to bury their dead. Now I looked out upon a great city of tombs, although 'tombs' does not do them justice. They were more like magnificent villas, with marble vaults and dry fountains. And all was in darkness now, which was just the way the dead like it, I imagine. Even in the long dark I could see that some of the tombs were marked with a pale white sign, the snake that eats its own tail. What had Tefnut said that it symbolised? Life swallowing life? Or death eating death? I hadn't been paying attention. I must confess that I've never been very taken with all of these new religious cults. If you ask me - you can't go far wrong with the Roman gods. Good old gods who don't get involved unless you do something to offend them. I said a quick prayer to Purrcury, the messenger of the gods, who is also God of Late Deliveries and Wrong Turns. Then I decided to leave the dead in their city and go back to join the living.

THE BIRDS

I'd turned tail, and started back up the track when the whiskers on my right side gave a little twitch. At first I thought they were playing up again but no, I could clearly sense a living presence, down amongst the dead and the cold marble. Unlike the Romans, we Kittons are not known for our natural inquisitiveness. So much so, that when the great Mewlius Caesar landed with his mighty invasion fleet, our tribe had no clue that we were at war until two weeks after the landing, when our chief's wife popped round to borrow a long ladder and a fishing rod.

Whatever was alive down amongst the tombs need not worry on my account. I had no plans to investigate. But I could not ignore the flutter of wings from a flock of tiny birds, flying about in circles around the dome of a mawsoleum. They flew straight at me, before stopping at the last moment and turning together, as if they were one great animal with a single mind. But not a particularly clear mind judging by the way that some of them were weaving about.

Then I sensed another presence on the path ahead. I did not need to sense for long for I soon caught scent of it. In the half-light, I saw a form moving in my direction. The worst thing had happened. I was staring at a snake. It was a great white snake, exactly like the pictures, except for two things. Its jaws were larger and it did not seem bothered about eating itself right now. Perhaps it had tired of the taste of its own tail. Its pale tongue shot out. Was it flicking for flies? It seemed to be tasting the air. It turned its great head towards me.

I struggled to remember my Gladiator training. Then it all came back to me. I turned and ran down the path as quickly as I could. But I knew I was running towards a dead end. There was no climbing down from that ledge. Tefnut had trained me in the thousand-year-old Fleagyptian fighting traditions. You might think that armed with this training, and my courage, I could expect to come through any trial. But there were certain problems. Firstly, I had only been trained to fight with a rake or a trident, and I didn't have either. Secondly, all the patterns that Tefnut had taught me in the Arena needed sand to make them work. And the floor of this cave was solid rock. Hadn't Tefnut said something about other moves in the Ring Raking tradition? Why in Peus' name hadn't I asked her to teach them to me!

As the Great Snake got closer, I could see that it wasn't a nice white colour, like fresh milk, but the dirty white of a thing that has spent many years underground eating filth. What dreadful pit had this horror slid from? Or had it been here forever? If it had its own religious cult, perhaps it wanted to be worshipped? Then a thought occurred to me.

I won't write down the prayer I said to the Great Snake, for I feel embarrassed thinking about it. However, I can safely say that the snake hadn't come down to the dead town to be worshipped. It had come here to feed. My prayers had no effect. I could see its forked tongue flicking, tasting the air again. I was close enough to see its eyes. Urrggh! They were white too! All I could think about was being eaten. The shame of it. With eyes shut tight, I prepared for the snake's jaws. I wondered if there would be poisoned fangs. The thought of poison made my coat crawl. So I tried to reason. I tried to remember the great thinkers of the Stroic philosophy. And that new one, where you search for the good in all creatures. But it was impossible. After a few seconds of hard searching, I could only come up with one good thing. At least eating Bathhausia's breakfasts has made me too big to be swallowed whole. Then, in a manner I found disgusting, the Great Snake unhinged its lower jaw and gaped at me. The stench from inside this pale horror was unspeakable. A dreadful mixture of smells that should not be mixed. I began to cough. My right whiskers twinged. It was the flutter of tiny wings. A flock of birds flew towards me, twisting and wheeling. Confused by the ledge, one bird missed her turn and crashed straight into the Great Snake's mouth. She would never see her nest again. The Great Snake accepted her with open jaws, like a gift. It never moved its gaze, not to the left or to the right. And at that moment, I knew that it was blind.

But snakes do not hunt by sight alone. The bird had only taken its attention for an instant. As it tasted the air to get my scent, I knew that my chance had come. Rake or no rake, I would use my Gladiator training to force my way past it.

So I pictured a ball of wool, getting smaller as it rolled down a slope. Why this thought came into my head, I cannot say. But it seemed better to die rolling than to lie quietly and wait for death's jaws. Holding this picture in my mind's eye, I began one of the 'patterns' that Tefnut had taught me back in the Arena. Each pattern was a series of movements and steps designed to confuse your opponent in the Arena. When repeated fluidly, they produced incredible results. Tefnut had called the pattern I was about to start 'The Bleached Bones' because it was a prayer to the poor old Sun god. There was no sun in here, but Fortune willing, I would live to see the light again if it worked its magic.

I began the pattern. A little leap forward, a dodge from left to right, and a few steps back and forth in a stop-start manner. I put in an extra sweep of the tail for good measure. Tefnut would not have approved of improvisation, but where was she when I needed her! I threw all my weight onto my left side and stumbled as if to fall as I rotated my body and rolled for all I was worth. I found myself rolling out, still in rhythm, past the head of the Great Snake.

I did not look back. I ran with the winged paws of Purrcury himself back up the path and away from the pale terror.

Is there more shame in being eaten by a blind snake than by a seeing one? I do not know. But I really owed Fortune this time. As if in acknowledgement, or as a lament to its fallen fellow, one bird gave off a cry. Clawdius would say it was a pawtent – a sign from the gods. But I had no time to puzzle over the meaning. The Moracle was gone and I had been recalled to the Imperial Palace.

WAY OUT

Back in the chamber, the Scenturian was happy to send a couple of his guards to escort me out of the cave. I can truly say that I have never been so glad to get out of a tourist attraction, although I doubt that the Villas of the Dead and the Great Pale Snake are in the brochure.

Of course I searched all around for Tefnut but there was no scent of her. The yard was deserted. The guides had all gone home because the Moracle cave was closed for the official period of mourning for the Emperor. No stallholder, however greedy, would dare to sell anything on a day like this. But when they reopened next week, there would be serious money to be made from selling souvenirs of the Emperor Tiberius.

Clawdius' wife Mogullania had called the palace 'a nest for vipers' but it was to the palace that I must now return. If my vision was right, the biggest viper of them all was Rome's new Emperor, and my new employer.

A NEW STAR

The sun was high in the sky by the time I got back to the Imperial Palace. As I approached the gates, the scene was incredible. It was as if Chaos had chased Mewpiter from his seat on Mount Olympuss. A great crowd was assembled, waiting for a glimpse of the new Emperor. One group of females were shouting:

"Little kitten! Hurrah for Rome's lovely little kit!"

Another, younger looking group shouted:

"Star! Rome has a new star!"

A third much larger group were shouting:

"Hail Caesar! fish and cream!"

It is said that the first two groups were made up of paid professionals. But the third group were genuine. It is traditional for the new Emperor to give out presents of free fish and cream. After what seemed like an age, I pushed my way through to the front of the crowd. When I gave my name, the old Spraetorian on the gate told me that Captain Matro was looking for me.

I OBEY THE CALL

Inside the palace, slaves, freedcats and citizens rushed in every direction, getting ready for the new Emperor. Fortune spun me a good one. The Emperor had not arrived yet. In fact he hadn't even been approved by the Senate yet. But it is as plain as a poor dog's dinner where the power lies in Rome. The Imperial cooks were already practising his favourite dishes. And whilst the Spraetorians drilled endlessly, a team of interior decorators were busy in the Imperial apartments for it is commonly known that the late Emperor Tiberius had unusual taste in furnishings and flooring. The mosaics in his guests' sleeping quarters were infamous. One was of a grinning shark with the inscription 'Bite Me!' picked out in gold tile. This fetched a high price at an auction held by the new Emperor.

I made my way immediately to my scribing room. I grabbed scroll and ink and ran like Purrcury to Captain Matro's office. In my haste, I forgot to knock before entering. I caught a glimpse of a white tail disappearing through the servant's flap in the far wall. There was a musky smell to the room.

When Captain Matro noticed me at the door, he tilted his head to the side and searched my eyes. Did he know that I'd left the palace without permission? Perhaps he'd had me followed?

"Spartapuss! Welcome," he began. Then he paused, in the way that trained speakers at the Senate do when they want to make the next thing they say sound important.

"Now Spartapuss, the time has come for you to earn your keep. Our new Emperor has called for you personally. And when he calls, we must obey."

On hearing this, my heart dropped a beat and I nearly dropped an inkpot over Matro's bearskin rug.

"That is a great honour Captain. But surely there is some other scribe here with more experience? I have only been here a week and I haven't done any actual scribing yet."

"Fear not, Gladiator!" purred Matro. "You are favoured by our new Emperor. It is said that you did him a great service in the Arena. Fortune was with you that day my friend. Take a drink and tell me of your great deeds at the Games."

He lent forward and lapped casually from a silver bowl.

"I can remember very little of that day," I replied.

"You are too modest, my friend. It is said that you saved the Emperor's life."

"There was an accident with a battle chariot. I helped to free the Emperor from the wreckage. But really, I would rather not speak of it," I replied.

Matro sensed my unease.

"Let us say no more about it. And as for the scribing, fear not. We will soon give you lines enough to loosen your writing paw, if not that modest tongue of yours."

And with that, the Captain of the Spraetorian guard signalled for me to leave. He would send word when the Emperor wanted me.

And so I am back in my room in the palace, writing my diary with a cursed collar stuck around my neck. There has been no word from Tefnut. The Emperor may summon me at any time. He has asked for me personally, but I suspect him of murder in cold blood. Dear Katrin was right – you take your life in your paws when you get yourself mixed up with the Imperial Family.

APURILIS XX

April 20th

Whenever I call, you must answer...

TODAY I WAS SUMMONED. As I hurried along the long corridor towards the Emperor's apartments, teams of decorators were already hard at work turning everything his favourite colour: pea green. They were complaining that old Tiberius had a fondness for painting everything a dreadful dark purple colour, 'Imperial Plum' I think it is called. So it took coats and coats of new paint to get rid of, and even then, the old colour left a dirty shadow that showed through. I wondered, when I meet the new Emperor, would he take one look at me and know that I am a witness to the murder that he ordered? Was the dead Emperor Tiberius just another old stain to be painted over?

Awaiting your fate is worse than the fate itself. It was almost a relief when I reached the door to the Emperor's chambers. You could tell that it was the Emperor's door because a couple of big Purrmanians were guarding it. The whiskers on my right side gave another little twinge. I must get a physician to take a look at that, I thought.

"State your name and your business with his Imperial Greatness!" growled the guard.

"I'm Spartapuss," I said. "And I've been summoned to do some scribing for the Emperor."

I held the scroll up for the guard to see and I tried to look casual. The guard looked surprised. No one was casual when they came to see the Emperor. He checked down his list and nodded when he came to my name.

"Spaaar-tapuss. Yes. In you go. Do not keep the Best and Greatest One waiting."

With a push from a paw the size of a dinner bowl, the door swung open.

There, with his paws up on a velvet cushion, sat Catligula. And wrapped around the thin neck of the Emperor of the Known World, was the 'witches' collar'. The coin on the collar was very like my own, only bigger and more important-looking. I half expected sparks or magic, with the two collars so close. But Catligula didn't even acknowledge my presence. He was busy gambling with his guests.

At the table sat a familiar face – Dogren of Purrmania. The other player was the Governor of Fleagypt, who had returned to Rome to meet his new Emperor. Gathered around a low table was an audience of attendants and guards, including Captain Matro.

Catligula flicked his tail expectantly. He looked like the cat who had got the cream and was working on getting the dog's dinner as well. He was playing his favourite game – Mice! And judging by the strained expressions of his two guests he was winning.

With an experienced flick of the paw, Catligula threw his mouse high into the air. It was a fresh young white one and it turned a neat somersault in mid air before landing hard on the board without a squeak. Then it stood perfectly still, exactly where it had landed.

"There! He stands in Mewpiter's square. Now give me my winnings. And don't forget Augustpuss' rule. I get an extra throw as my mouse did not take a step when he landed."

"You have uncommonly good fortune, Caesar," said the Governor of Fleagypt (who had never heard of this rule before). "That is the seventh time your mouse has landed right way up in Mewpiter's house, without a step or a squeak."

The Governor suspected that Catligula was cheating. It did not bother him to lose money to the Emperor. Fleagypt was the richest province in the whole empire. This was just another form of tax. Whatever he lost at Mice today would be money well spent. In fact he wished they could skip the games. He would rather have given Catligula the money and got it over with.

"The gods favour you, Caesar Best and Greatest," said Dogren as he surrendered another gold coin from his pile.

"Of course they do," smiled Catligula, kissing his pile of winnings and giving one of Dogren's whiskers a hard tweak. They were as thick as goose feathers.

"Where did you get all of that gold from, Dogren my friend?" laughed the Governor. "Rome must be paying her soldiers too much."

Catligula gazed at Dogren's pile of gold coins.

Dogren laughed a half laugh and scratched his battle-torn ear.

"Answer him," said Catligula.

Dogren's gruff voice grew higher when he answered.

"Caesar, this money was a gift from you. When you became Emperor, you had me pay the Purrmanian Bodyguards two hundred a cat for their loyalty. Can't you remember?"

"Your Caesar always remembers," said Catligula. "It was very generous of me, wasn't it? I bet that old dog Tiberius wasn't as generous." Catligula gripped his mouse and drew back his paw to throw again.

"Actually, I remember he paid his Bodyguards five hundred in gold per tail," said the soon to be ex-Governor of Fleagypt.

Catligula paused in mid-throw and dropped his mouse, like a dog that has found a better stick.

"Do you play any good games in Fleagypt Governor? I grow tired of this one," Catligula asked in a low voice.

LET HIM ROLL

Dogren didn't need to sense the sudden change in his master's mood because Catligula's expression said everything. It is whispered that Catligula spends an hour every day in front of the mirror, practising his dread expressions. This one was cold and cruel with a helping of loathing in it. The Governor sat stock-still and he would have liked to blend into the background, but the pea green and gold walls made blending in difficult.

"We play exactly the same games as you play here in Rome, Caesar," said the Governor. "The same games and the same rules," he added with a diplomatic smile.

"Let us be honest and speak freely," said Catligula sweetly. "You think that I am playing with loaded mice, don't you?"

"Why of course not Caesar..." coughed the Governor, but his eyes gave him away. They were fixed on the mosaic floor and try as he might, he could not meet Catligula's terrible gaze.

"Speak the truth. You think your Emperor is a cheat. You only play because you are afraid of me," said Catligula.

"No Caesar! It is not like that at all," choked the Governor.

"And now you lie to your Emperor," said Catligula.

The Governor said nothing. He just shook his head. His wife had warned him to watch his behaviour but it had been a long feast and there had been catnip treats for dessert.

"Well Dogren, since your Emperor's mouse cannot be trusted, we had better find a more reliable mouse for this game," said Catligula with a wild smile.

"Seize him!" he ordered. In an instant Dogren had

the Governor's head pressed down hard against the marble floor.

"It's your throw Dogren. And mark carefully whether or not he moves on the landing because I will have no cheating!" said Catligula.

Dogren hurled the Governor up into the air. He landed awkwardly, breaking an ornamental vase.

"He moved on purpose! That's a no-throw. Tie his paws together and throw him again!" said Catligula.

The game went on and on. But the Governor made no sound and did not plead. Like all Roman officials he had served his time in the legions and knew that it never paid to protest a punishment. It was better to accept whatever throws the gods had in store for you. Eventually they would grow weary of toying with you.

But Catligula was still enjoying the toying. Throw after throw passed. Finally, he trotted over to where the crumpled body of the Governor was lying.

"Are you dead yet?" asked Catligula.

With an enormous effort, the once proud Governor of Fleagypt strained and lifted his tail.

"Oh well," said the Emperor of the Known World. "One more throw will decide all. "Look everyone! Mark carefully where he lands. My mosaic floor shall be the game board that decides his fate."

Catligula pressed his nose against the Governor's battered face.

"If you land in the green, you can have your life. But if you fall on black..."

Purrmanians, slaves, Spraetorians and I all looked on as Catligula gave the command and Dogren hurled the Governor into the air once more.

Without the strength to right himself, he fell head-first onto the tiles with a crack. He looked up at the Emperor. But Catligula had turned away.

"In Peus' name, I missed it!" said Catligula, calling Captain Matro to his side.

"Spraetorian! You be our referee. Did he land upon the black tiles or the green?" asked Catligula earnestly. "Speak truly for his life is in the balance!" he added with a yawn.

Matro's tail gave a little flick. I knew that like me, he was horrified by this cruel display. But for either of us to speak out would mean the risk of changing places with the broken prisoner.

Eventually the captain answered.

"I believe he landed on green Caesar."

All eyes in the room were on Catligula, which was exactly where he wanted them.

"Now, what did I say the green tiles stood for? Was it life or death?"

The whole room gasped. Without realising what I was doing I heard my own voice saying,

"Was it green for life Caesar? Green is the colour of life in Fleagypt."

The Governor rolled upon his back.

Catligula scratched at his collar and turned towards me.

"We are in Rome now," he said. "But I have always bet on the green team at the chariot races. So Governor, you are allowed to live. Now thank me and leave. Unless you'd care for another game?"

As Dogren untied him, the Governor sobbed his thanks and clawed his way towards the door. At first the attendants were afraid to help him. But Matro ordered a couple of Spraetorians to carry him out.

"Tell the Senate that I need a new Governor to rule Fleagypt. The old one has lost his leap," said Catligula. At this, the whole room laughed.

THE CAPTAIN'S WARNING

Catligula said nothing further to me that night. He did not leave until dawn, by which time Dogren had lost every coin. Generous as ever, Catligula made him accept a loan. As I was leaving, Captain Matro called me to his office. His tone was friendly. He told me that my first task was to write down Catligula's words on the occasion of the funeral of the Emperor Tiberius. He could see that I looked nervous but did his best to put me at my ease.

"It could not be simpler Spartapuss," he said. "All you have to do is take down exactly what the Emperor says."

"Yes Captain," I replied.

"But be a historian about it. Tidy the speech up a bit and put in a good phrase or two here and there. We must to make Caesar come across better. Not that there is anything wrong... But we must make him sound more..."

There was a pause. Matro rolled his eyes upwards as if the right words were to be found in the heavens.

"More sympathetic?" I suggested.

The captain smiled. At last I felt that there was an understanding between us. Then I swore that he could rely on me. He gave me his thanks and dismissed me. I started to leave, but as I reached the door he stopped me.

"Spartapuss, you spoke bravely tonight in front of the Emperor. But you would be wise to remember never to speak to him unless he asks you a question. You don't want to end up in his bad books."

There was something about the way that he said this last phrase that troubled me. I left the room wondering how long I would last in my new job.

Back in my room, I took to my cushion and tried to make sense of the day. Catligula was fickle. He could turn at any moment. Yet, I reasoned, hadn't he excused me from the law that forbids a servant to speak to an Emperor? Had he remembered that I'd saved his life at the Games of Purrcury? Perhaps I would be safe until I could find some way to get the collar off.

But in all these thoughts I was only as wise as the moth that turns in circles around the bright candle, thinking that he has found the moon. Tonight I had seen with my own eyes how dangerous it is for those who stand too close to the flame.

The Official History of the Emperor Gattus Tiberius ('Catligula') as told to his scribe by the Best and Greatest one himself

The Emperor's words upon the occasion of the State Funeral of the late and dear Emperor Tiberius, were as follows,
"As I sit in comfort with a reasonable view of this funeral procession, I overlook one of the saddest scenes that I have ever overlooked. Vast crowds of you are following the hearse to the temple of Mewpiter. There, the ex-Emperor Tiberius will be laid to rest. Old Tibbles ruled Rome with an iron paw, all on his own, unless you count the many interferences of his mother Mewlia. I know that Tiberius didn't show much love for her in public. But I also know that the rumour that he had her poisoned is a false one. Anyone heard repeating this lie will find themselves scrubbing the municipal litter tray with their own torn-out tongue for a brush.
As I look down on the crowds of simple citizens padding along behind old Tibbles' hearse, I feel close to you. Close to your grief. Close enough, in some cases, to tell exactly what you had for your breakfasts. And indeed, I would be mourning with you

if I didn't have to stay here in the palace all morning to make sure that the painters arc carrying out my instructions. They are as slippery as swamp eels with their estimates. But as I sit up here lapping my cream, it strikes me that old Tiberius never really understood quite how you felt about him. Perhaps you were too afraid for your own lives to tell your Emperor honestly just how feared and respected he was. But if he looks down on you now, as I do, he will understand. Your fear and awe were always followed by your affection – like a lean wolf stalking two fat sheep. In one of the rooms here at the palace, there are more than ten thousand scrolls sent in all over our great Empire. Among the requests for him to lower taxes are many "Thank you for sparing us!" scrolls from tribes he conquered. And that just goes to show the huge appeal he had, to the great untrained hordes that he ruled over. Now it is the duty of those of you that he allowed to live, to keep him alive in your memories."

APURILIS XXII

April 22nd

The Smell of It

Today a Spraetorian arrived with a message. I was summoned to meet Captain Matro in his office. There was something familiar in the air all down the corridor. I was soon to find out the reason. It was the musky perfume that Mogullania had worn at Spatopia. The name of this perfume was Smell. It is imported from Cathens in unusually shaped bottles with the inscription 'Ah! The Smell of It!' on them. What the Cathenians made this scent out of, I do not know. Boiled up whales and porpoises perhaps? I was coughing as I entered the room but Matro and his guest did not notice.

"Are you trying to buy me off?" hissed a voice high enough to trouble dogs. Mogullania shot out a paw and knocked an object from Matro's grasp. It landed hard on the marble floor. It was a diamond collar.

"It is humiliating enough being seen in public with that half-witted husband of mine. An evening of feasting with the rest of the Senate sniffing at me would be intolerable."

"I fear the Emperor's mind cannot be changed. He commands you and Clawdius to attend," said Matro.

"Then make something up!" hissed Mogullania. "Tell him Clawdius is foaming at the mouth again."

"I cannot my love..." started Matro.

Although it is not polite to listen at doorways, it is hard to stop once you've started. But before I could leave, the door swung fully open. Captain Matro looked fierce. On his cushion sat Mogullania, with a face as sour as week-old cream in summer.

On the floor in front of her was Matro's present, a diamond collar.

"You! What are you doing here?" spat Mogullania.

"I was summoned" I replied.

"Spartapuss, leave us," said Captain Matro.

As I turned to leave he added:

"You will say nothing to the Emperor about what you have seen here."

It was a command, not a request.

APURILIS XXIII

April 23rd

Fleanus' Paw

So I HAVE WITNESSED my first Imperial scandal! The paths of love are strange. Captain Matro and Mogullania! The goddess Fleanus has a fickle paw. I passed the Captain on the way to dinner but he stalked straight past me without a second glance. What he can smell in her, I do not know. But it is often said that 'beauty is in the nose of the beholder'.

There is still no word from Tefnut. Being a mystic, she has probably gone off on some business somewhere else and forgotten all about me.

APURILIS XXIV

April 24th

The Book of the Dagger

TODAY I SURVIVED another audience with Catligula. His banquet was unexpectedly cancelled.

There are two very good reasons to be early for an Imperial Dinner. Firstly, the cooks always send out the biggest portions first in order to look good in front of the Emperor. Secondly, it is rude to arrive late unless you are fashionable. No wonder the fashionable always look so thin.

So I arrived at the Imperial Apartments at the appointed time, bringing my scribing materials with me. To my horror, I found that none of the other guests had arrived. I found Catligula reclining on his cushioned throne. I nearly choked when I saw what he was doing. Reading has never formed a part of the Imperial Education. Why read a book yourself when you can have it read to you? That is not to say that the Imperials are not well-educated. They have the best tutors that money can buy to teach them public speaking. And the best tutors write the best essays when it comes to examination time.

So I was amazed to see Catligula taking such pains to read for himself. He seemed impatient and he kept rolling and unrolling the scroll. From time to time he scratched at his neck violently and sent the great gold coin on his collar spinning on its fastenings.

I watched for some time, waiting for him to speak. I had remembered Matro's warning not to speak to the Emperor unless spoken to. But the Emperor said nothing, so neither did I. Knowing what I know, was it surprising that his collar had such a fascination for me? My eyes were drawn towards it and it was all I could do the resist the urge to scratch at my own collar. Whether this was because of some strange magic or from something I had picked up from one of the kitchen workers, I cannot say.

Catligula yawned. Flipping the scroll back into its case, he looked up and acknowledged me.

"You summoned me, Emperor," I said.

"Yes I did, didn't I?" said Catligula.

His face, which had been fixed in one of his serious scowls, seemed to brighten. Was he playing with me? His thin eyes weren't giving away any secrets. It was so quiet that I could hear the wax run down the torches. Catligula leaned forward, "They told you not to speak to me, didn't they?" he said.

There was nothing to do but nod.

"Fools! You may speak freely with your Emperor."

My mind was not blank. It was stuffed full of the many things that I knew I should not mention. I tried to look anywhere but into his eyes or at his collar.

Finally, I noticed the scroll that he had been reading. The case was red with a long dagger on the cover.

"I see you are reading Caesar," I began. "Is it any good?"

"Is it any good?!!!" said Catligula, laughing the kind of laugh you hear in the theatre and nearly shaking himself off his cushion.

He beckoned at me to approach.

"Written here is a list of names. Come, have a good look. Do you know any of them?"

I read a tail's length down the scroll. Amongst those named were a couple of very well known senators. One name stood out – the philosopher Pusspero, the richest cat in Rome (from an old family who had been in slow decline until a clever grandfather made a killing selling a new type of flea comb).

"I don't know any of them personally, Caesar. I have recently been freed and besides, I have a terrible memory."

"This is a list of my enemies. They think I am a newborn kitten, with my eyes not yet open. But I see everything. That is why, whenever I want, they must die."

There was a moment of silence.

"Is that why you have a dagger on the cover?" I asked.

With wild eyes, he picked up the scroll and drew out a hidden blade. It was thin with something dark and sticky at the tip.

"With this blade, they will take their own lives, whenever I order it. But not yet. It shall be our secret."

"Yes Caesar," I replied, wondering what the sticky stuff on the blade could be.

"Why do you think I'm telling you this?" asked Catligula, stroking his collar.

I had no idea what to say, even if my very life depended on it (which of course, it did).

"I cannot say Caesar. I'm just a simple freedcat, new to the job of scribing."

"But we understand each other, do we not?" purred Catligula. He stroked his collar again. It was all that I could do to prevent myself from stroking my own collar. By a great effort of will I stopped myself and managed to smile. I wished that a big hole would open up in the middle of his oceanic mosaic and I could swim off or crawl under a rock.

"Your Emperor never forgets," he began, "at the Games of Purrcury my chariot turned over and I was pinned, with my poor leg trapped. There were many on that day that sat on their fat paws and did nothing to help. They would have let me die. But that can never be. And now I have their names, in my little book."

I nodded. The storm had passed as quickly as it had come on.

"Fortune sent you to my side that day. Go! I will call for you, when I need you."

He smiled and took up his pen to damn some other poor unfortunate. Then he changed his mind, reached under his cushion and produced a wooden box marked with a symbol that I could not miss — the white snake that eats itself.

I had been dismissed, so I had to leave. Glancing back I saw him open the box. I could not see what was inside. Whatever was in that box had Catligula's full attention that evening. The Emperor's guests were not best pleased to hear that dinner was cancelled, as most had travelled a long way. And they had been told to leave their gifts at the palace. Tomorrow they would have the expense of buying new gifts. But now they would have to go to the trouble of finding a cushion for the night. And I must retire to mine with a question on my mind. What does Catligula keep inside that box?

APURILIS XXV

April 25th

Dinner at Caesar's

THERE HAVE BEEN MANY DISASTROUS DINNERS down the ages, but tonight Catligula dished up an absolute horror. His latest game started well enough, with the guests arriving exactly on time. However, Catligula would not let anyone into his apartments save for Mogullania, Clawdius and myself. Everyone else was told to form a queue outside and be ready with their admission fee and gifts. He was charging two in gold per tail to get in. We were ushered in by Captain Matro, who was immaculately turned out as usual. He had the disinterested look that you see in all the best restaurants in Rome. Clawdius congratulated him on it, telling him that he looked as if he had been waiting expensive tables all his life. Mogullania scowled and told Clawdius to be silent.

"Welcome to Caesar's Imperial Dining Room," said Captain Matro. Dinner for two is it? Wait here and I will find you a table."

Mogullania nodded. As he left, Matro stole a glance at Mogullania. Clawdius' wife was no Helen of Tray. At the Spa someone once said that her face would launch a thousand ships – in the other direction. This was unkind, for although her markings were heavy and her head was perhaps a little over large for her body, she was always perfectly groomed.

I waited at a respectful distance behind Clawdius and Mogullania. By the time Matro returned, Mogullania was growling about the 'poor service'. She was interrupted by a familiar voice.

"The service here at Caesar's is excellent my dear. Far better than the guests deserve," said Catligula.

Mogullania flicked her tail and stared right through

the Emperor.

"From what I hear, you've already rubbed up against our Head Waiter, Captain Matro here," said Catligula.

By her furious scowl, Mogullania was ready with a reply. But the Emperor wasn't used to be being interrupted. He would not let her get a word in.

"That's a nice new diamond collar you're wearing my dear. A present, was it? From someone special?" As he said this, Catligula looked right past Clawdius towards Captain Matro.

Mogullania stared at Matro in amazement. Matro said nothing. Mogullania began to bristle as her embarrassment turned to fury. Mercifully, at this point Matro broke the silence.

"Your table awaits," he said with the battle-proven calm of a soldier. Then he led the unhappy couple away to their places.

But Catligula wasn't finished yet. Following along, he turned to Clawdius and asked:

"Uncle, you two don't mind sitting with Spartapuss here do you? I believe you all know each other and we're going to be short of cushions when that lot from the Senate arrive."

Clawdius smiled and said that he was sure it would be all right. Mogullania turned her nose up, as if I was a piece of week-old meat that had been left to fester on the plate. She turned to Clawdius.

"How can you agree to dine with this freedcat

who you have dismissed from your service? Is it fitting for us to eat with an unemployed Gladiator? You are shaming me, once again."

But Catligula, who had excellent hearing, smiled and said:

"Fear not my dear. He is not unemployed. I have given him a job, as my Imperial Scribe. He's taking down everything that is said and for my Glorious Résumé."

"Caesar is writing a history of his deeds. He's going to have it carved on the walls of all the major temples in Rome," explained Matro.

Clawdius went along with all of this, saying that Catligula's history of himself sounded absolutely fascinating. But the Emperor knew when he was being humoured.

"I hope you don't mind me employing your ex-slave, uncle," said Catligula in a whisper loud enough for the theatre. "It looks bad if we Clawdians can't look after our own freedcats. You can't go freeing them and abandoning them. They might turn, and go feral."

This last line was directed at Mogullania.

Clawdius smiled. Catligula grabbed a gong from a passing waiter and banged it enthusiastically.

"Service! Service in the VIP section!" he shouted, padding off towards some senators who were arriving.

Then our 'waiter' arrived. Dogren of Purrmania, once the terror of the Neuterberger Forest, consulted his table plan and showed us to our places. Clawdius shuffled to his cushion as Mogullania hissed under her breath that the rat catcher had cleaner cutlery than this.

"Apologies from the house," said Dogren, picking up her knife and giving it a good lick. With a leathery paw that was happier wielding a battle-axe than cleaning cutlery, he polished the knife and set it down on the table.

"For you Sir, the house recommends the bowl of mixed meats or the eel plate," said Dogren. I chose the eel plate and Clawdius went for the meats as usual.

"I'll have a bowl of water," said Mogullania coldly.

"Water?" said Catligula, who had returned from worrying the other guests.

"Uncle, tell your wife to order something. This is supposed to be a fund-raiser for my next Games."

Clawdius began to splutter and cough but no words came out. Mogullania looked at him in disgust.

"A bowl of cold water please. I have no appetite for anything else here," she hissed.

Catligula's eyes flashed.

"Emperor, I have a headache," said Mogullania with all the politeness she could manage. "I want to go home, if I am allowed?"

The other diners fell silent. Most of them knew only too well what happened when you crossed Catligula.

"As you wish, my dear," said Catligula.

"Off you g-go and sleep it off my darling," said Clawdius, relieved.

"But before she goes she must sign my Guest Book," said Catligula. He began to scratch at his collar excitedly as if to rid himself of a flea.

Dogren was sent off to fetch it.

"Make sure she signs it uncle," said Catligula.

"Everyone who leaves early must write their comments. And sign their name," he added.

And with that he went away to terrorise another table.

Mogullania looked through Clawdius as if he was a stray dog. She took up the pen and unrolled the scroll. There, on the cover was a red dagger with a long tip.

"Wait!" I heard myself whisper. "Mogullania, it is very early. It would be better to stay."

But she wasn't listening. Twice she put pen to paper but stopped without writing anything. No doubt she was thinking up something really clever.

"Mogullania, in Peus' name please don't put your name in there!" I said.

Clawdius must have caught something in the tone of my voice. He struggled to get his words out. When the words didn't come, he snatched the pen from Mogullania, gathered up the scroll and gave it back to Dogren saying:

"Waiter, she's c-changed her mind. She's staying for dinner."

As he passed the book back to Dogren, Clawdius made sure that Mogullania got a good look at the red dagger on the cover.

"What will it be Madam?" growled Dogren, not prepared for this change of plan.

"She'll have the Eel Plate, it's always been her f-favourite," said Clawdius.

Mogullania scowled and opened her mouth to speak. But Fortune must have held her tongue for at that moment she realised what was happening.

"Yes – one Eel Plate please," she purred.

Dogren took the order and Clawdius breathed a sigh of relief. When Mogullania looked at him, I saw something unusual in her gaze, somewhere between loathing and pity. But as we were about to find out, the evening still had a sting in it. When Dogren returned, he was not carrying food.

"The Emperor asks if you would like to see the Special Menu?" he said.

"No t-thank you," spluttered Clawdius. "We are honoured just to b-be here. We have no need of special treatment."

"As you wish," said Dogren. And he lumbered off towards the kitchen to fetch our food, taking his Special Menu with him.

A COLD DISH

Whatever his wife and the rest of Rome may think, Clawdius is no half-wit. And it was to prove well for Mogullania she'd followed her husband's advice. It is said that 'revenge is a dish best served cold' and Catligula had given his cooks careful instructions based on a book he had stolen from a locked chest, hidden in his great grandmother's private apartment.

He was to serve up many special dishes from her cookbook that night.

Until now he had not acted against his enemies in the Senate. So here they were. All those who had whispered about him behind his back. They were the cream of Roman society, so accustomed to luxury and special treatment that they expected it. So whenever they complained about the food they were offered the Special Menu. It was full of delights like field mice tails in fish liquor, sheep's livers on grass, sea slugs served in their own juice. But each of these dishes had its own special ingredient. Some of the poisons took time to work and others worked quickly. There were tasteless poisons that were undetectable, save for a slight numbness on the victim's tongue. Others made their victims choke or stopped their hearts. And all through this deadly feast, Catligula ordered his waiters to continue to serve food and act as if nothing were happening. The unfortunates fell face first into their bowls or rolled on their bellies. The guests became terrified and refused to eat their 'specials'. But Catligula gave Dogren instructions to let no one leave the feast until every plate was licked clean.

APURILIS XXVII

April 27th

Loose Tongues

THREE DAYS HAVE NOW PASSED since the Emperor's dinner. The morning after that terrible meal, there were thirty empty cushions at the Senate. These are to be filled by supporters of the Emperor. Far from turning against Catligula, the mob love him more each day. This morning I awoke to the sound of a cheering crowd outside the palace gates. He has announced that he is bringing back the free fish. Clawdius was always against this. Firstly because it put a great strain on the public purse but secondly because it meant that every stray from here to Purrmania headed towards Rome to get their free ration every day.

This morning Captain Matro had some strong words for me, which I shall not record here. He said that I had broken my word to him and betrayed his trust. I tried to explain that I said nothing to Catligula about him and Mogullania, but he would not believe me. How else could Catligula know about the diamond collar that he gave her? Nobody else had seen them together. When I promised him that no word of it had passed my lips he lectured me about what they do to spies in the legions. Apparently, they pull their tongues out after first loosening them on a special machine.

I decided to cheer myself up with a dinner. But

when my roasted cod arrived, I could not bear to look at its great lips and glassy eyes gazing up at me from the bowl. Although the canteen was busy, I was left with a table to myself. Gossip travels fast in this palace. Strangers dare not speak to me, for it is said that I am the Emperor's pet and cannot hold my tongue. Nobody has said a word to me today. The only contact I have had came from an old Spraetorian who spat at me, and a Fleagyptian servant who muttered something as I passed her in the kitchen. I'm sure she was either mad or sick.

APURILIS XXVIII

April 28th

Over My Head

LAST NIGHT I FELL INTO STRANGE DREAMS. First I dreamed of eagles flying over the palace. Then, like a scene at the theatre, my dream changed. Catligula opened a box and from it, all the evils of the world poured out upon the city. About an hour before dawn, I woke with a start. I sprang to the shutters and looked out. The whiskers on my right side were playing me up. The only light came from the Spraetorian guards' fire, far away by the gates, like a small ship on a great dark ocean.

Had my ears deceived me? Perhaps I'd heard a bird

on the roof, for they are always trying to break in there and rob the walls of materials for nest-building. I sat still and decided to watch for a while. It was not long before I was dreaming again. A familiar voice whispered:

"Spartapuss, wake up."

I jumped to the window again and looked but there was absolutely no sign of anyone outside. The voice was coming straight out of the night air.

"Tefnut? Is that you?" I said, feeling foolish.

I began to wonder whether I was hearing her spirit.

Or perhaps she had made her body disappear, with some strange charm out of the East.

"Tefnut? Have you made yourself invisible?" I asked.

"No," came the reply. "I am lying on the roof above your window. Do not look up. It is a matter of great importance that you do not see me."

Here we were again. The riddles had started.

"'Most important that you do not see me?'" "Well, you've been doing a good job of avoiding me these last weeks," I replied. Perhaps this was a little unfair but I was pleased with myself for thinking up a good reply in the flick of a tail. Tefnut ignored it.

"Are you still wearing what you call the 'witches' collar'?" she asked. For the first time since we'd met I could hear the impatience in her voice.

"Of course I'm still wearing it. I cannot get it off!" I hissed.

"Then whatever you see, Catligula can see too," said Tefnut. "And it is most important that he never finds out about me or my business here."

At first I didn't understand, and even when she'd explained, I didn't know what to think. Tefnut told me that the Emperor was using me. He'd been seeing through my eyes by means of the wretched 'witches' collar', which was stuck around my neck. She reminded me of the riddle I heard at the Moracle cave.

'Wherever you go, I will be,
Whatever you see, I can see,
Whenever I call, you must answer,
Until I'm undone, you will never be free.'

The Emperor had already seen a lot through me. And it had made me into a figure of hate at the palace. In my despair I cried out:

"Why in Peus' name does everything have to be so difficult! Why do we need to spy through the eyes of others? Why can't we just be reasonable?"

But I didn't need a mystic teacher to point out that it was no use expecting the Imperials to be reasonable. It was against their nature. Tefnut waited politely for me to finish before answering in a grave voice.

"Spartapuss, I come to you now at great risk and against the advice of the wise. You have put yourself in peril by getting so close to the Emperor. You would do well to be more distant. Behave like a servant, not like a friend."

"But I can't help it if he wants to be my friend," I replied, feeling friendless.

"And besides, if he summons me I have to attend."

Tefnut said nothing. I think I'd interrupted her in the middle of a lecture that she'd been rehearsing for a while and now she had lost her place. Finally she continued.

"Yes, you must attend to him. But several times you have spoken when it would have been better to keep your mouth closed."

In Peus' name this was unfair especially coming from Tefnut, who had abandoned me to fend for myself.

"But if he sees everything that I see, what is the difference? There is nothing I can do about it!"

"You spoke up for the Fleagyptian Governor, and warned Clawdius' wife against eating from the special menu. These were kind actions but dangerous."

She was right again. I was sick of being in the wrong.

"Where were you at the Moracle cave?" I demanded in a half hiss. "I waited for you, but you never came. What was I supposed to do?"

But there was no answer from the roof. Finally she whispered,

"Spartapuss. There is little time. Listen to me. I have come because the Moracle has been taken."

"I know," I said, for once feeling rather pleased with myself.

After a short pause, to sweeten the meat as they say,

I told Tefnut what had happened in the Moracle cave. I got as far as the part where I'd seen the Spraetorians wheeling away the Moracle's house. But when it came to telling of my encounter with the Great White Snake, something held my tongue.

When my tale was over, she was silent. Over by the gate the Spraetorians were changing their watch. The darkest part of the night was over.

"We must get her back," said Tefnut. "Catligula still has her somewhere in the palace."

I have never been known as a very quick thinker. Katrin once said that my mind is running a marathon, not a sprint. But I had an idea. Somehow, I instinctively knew where Catligula would be keeping the Moracle – in the box marked with the sign of the Great White Snake. It must have come from the Moracle cave. I was delighted. I, Spartapuss had solved the riddle and a difficult one at that. But as I opened my mouth to speak, the whole room shook as if Paws himself had summoned up a great earthquake.

The door rocked on its hinges.

"Open the door!" growled a voice. "Who's there?" was the best reply I could muster. I imagined Tefnut rolling her eyes to the heavens.

"Open up! You are commanded to attend the Emperor," came the reply.

I began to explain to whoever it was that my door was kept bolted shut at night and if they wanted the key, they would have to get it from Captain Matro.

With a crack, the solid oak door splintered into pieces and Dogren of Purrmania squeezed his great bulk into the room.

"So Captain Matro keeps Caesar's pet locked up at night?" said Dogren. It was not said with particular menace – you knew about it if Dogren wanted to be menacing. His orders were to bring me to the Emperor immediately.

I had no clue what to make of this summons. Surely Catligula had no need of a scribe at this hour?

"Be quick," said Dogren as I grabbed my writing materials. "It is a matter of the greatest importance."

There was concern in his voice. I asked him what was wrong. Turning around to check that no one was listening, Dogren stooped and lent closer to me.

"It is Caesar. There is something wrong with his dreams," he said.

THE CHAMBER

When I entered the Imperial chamber, I found the Emperor in a terrible state. He'd piled up every possession in the room in front of his door. I had never seen him afraid before. He crouched in the corner, clutching the box with the white snake on the lid.

The Emperor seemed relived to see me.

"Are they gone?" he asked, looking towards his windows.

"Look for me. For I cannot..."

"Yes Caesar" I said quietly. As I approached, I saw

that all the windows had been nailed shut.

"Why were they shouting?" asked the ruler of the known world.

"The crowd gathered because they are happy about the free fish," I answered. "But they have mostly gone now, for it is too early for celebrating."

"Are you sure?" he replied, looking anxiously towards the window, his body low to the ground.

He scratched nervously at his collar and shot a look towards the window.

"I saw eagles," he whispered. "They were coming to carry me away."

"That must have been a dream Caesar. It's a supposed to be a good pawtent, to dream of eagles. The eagle is the king of the birds. And you're the ruler of Rome. They were probably just coming to greet you."

I knew I was talking nonsense, Matro had warned me to choose every word with care in the Emperor's presence. Now Catligula was curious.

"Scribe, do you ever dream?" he asked.

"Sometimes..." I began.

"Did you dream tonight?" he asked urgently.

"I believe so Caesar, but I cannot say for certain, for I was asleep at the time."

Beckoning me towards him, he leaned closer and whispered.

"Tell me scribe, what did you dream about tonight?"

I thought before I answered. I knew what not to

mention. I could not tell him of my own dream where he himself had opened the box with the snake, and let out all the evils of the world. And I knew that his friendship was brittle. He could turn in an instant. So I said:

"I am sorry Caesar but I can never remember my dreams. I try but I forget them the instant I wake up. All my people, from the tribes of the Kittons, are exactly the same."

This was a lie, but I put my whole self into it. I remembered the words of the training manual of Spatopia, where it says that believing yourself is the key to making the customers believe you.

The Emperor looked towards the window again, perhaps searching for eagles.

"I am sorry Caesar. It is said that we Kittons have fur for brains," I added.

Catligula pulled at the collar around his neck and drew it tight. By all the gods on Mount Olympuss, it was as if someone was tightening my own collar. The force was enough to start me choking. I struggled to draw breath and then again to push the air out of my lungs. Finally his stopped pulling at his collar and let me go. My own collar grew looser and I could breath freely once more.

"Fur for brains?" he said with a flick of the tail. "Well scribe, from now on you will write down your dreams for me."

Before I could answer, he ordered me to leave, turned around and started digging in a pile of cushions. As I padded out I stole a look back. From the corner of my eye I saw him stroking the lid of the snake box.

It seemed to give him comfort. I could smell something in that box, a scent that took me back to the Moracle cave. I could not wait to bring the news to Tefnut. But when I returned to my room she had gone.

APURILIS XXX

April 30th

Strange Dreams

IN THE HOPE of avoiding another choking, I have started writing my dream diary for Catligula. I have got another scroll for this purpose. No doubt Tefnut would not approve but what choice do I have?

When the Emperor Tiberius fell out with the dream interpreters and banned them from the city it only served to encourage the amateurs. Back at Spatopia the customers were always going on about their dreams. It was enough to put anyone to sleep. The usual dreams were about endlessly chasing after a mouse that always stays a whisker out of paw's reach. Or climbing down from a great tree but never reaching the ground. So I shall stick to this material and not record anything that might excite Catligula.

The Dream Diary of Spartapuss, scribe to the Emperor. Part I

Last night I dreamed about a rat that ran away. I tried to catch it and eat it but I could not. It ran away again. I chased it again. It ran. I chased. It ran. And then I woke up.

MAIUS I

May 1st

Leave Nothing Out

T HE SPRAETORIAN returned again this morning for my dream diary. But when I unrolled the scroll to start writing about last night, I saw that the Emperor had torn it half to pieces and crossed out what I had written yesterday.

Underneath this, in his own writing, I read the words:

RATS! TELL ME EVERY DETAIL. AND TELL ME WHAT YOU THINK YOUR DREAMS MEAN. LEAVE NOTHING OUT.

So I have decided that it is safest to give him more detail and perhaps take inspiration from the truth. I sent the Spraetorian away and began another entry.

The Dream Diary of Spartapuss, scribe to the Emperor Part II

I am Spartapuss and these are my dreams.

I dreamed that I was going to the Senate. When I padded up the steps I saw the Spraetorians outside so I knew that the Senators were in the middle of a debate. But as I drew nearer, instead of the usual hisses, I heard a great scrabbling, and the unmistakable sound of gnawing.

When I looked in through the great doors, I saw that the Senate was packed full of rats. Instead of flying at their throats, the Spraetorians were guarding them carefully. They were very neatly turned out in their little collars there was no tail biting in evidence. Now and again one of them would run across the floor in the middle of the speech. Any observer would agree that these rats were far better behaved than our own senators. They had just passed a law about widening the sewer pipes to make it easier for many rats to pass at the same time and avoid a dangerous crush. There were passionate speeches for and against. They were about to debate a motion to double the cheese ration when I awoke.

INTERPRETATION: There has been a lot of rat activity recently in the roof above my sleeping place. I cannot stand the thought of them running around up there. This dream tells me that it is best to leave them alone. Rats are making a good job of running their own affairs.

The ink was still drying on my dream diary when the Spraetorian arrived to take it to Catligula.

MAIUS II

May 2nd

Do it Clean

THERE HAS BEEN NO WORD from the Emperor about my second rats dream. He has summoned me for some official scribing later this evening. So once again I have time to take up my real diary, which already contains stranger reports than my dream diary.

I'm worried about prying eyes here at the palace. Yesterday I answered an unexpected knock to find a young cleaner at my door. She said she had been sent to clear up the mess around my writing desk. I was about to send her away as usual. I do not like anyone 'cleaning' around my desk because it is well known that there are spies here at the palace. But there was something familiar about her face. I asked her if we'd met before and she answered no. She said that her name was Neferkitti. There was something familiar about that name too but I could not place it. She begged me to let her come in and at least give the desk a quick going over. She said she would get into trouble if it were left in this state. With so many papers and scrolls around it would attract any mice in the area looking for a nesting spot. Then she quoted some regulation that had just been introduced.

Not wanting to get her into trouble, I agreed to let her give it a quick 'lick and polish' while I went out to get some ink. I pretended to leave the room in a hurry but I crept slowly back in and pounced. I found her going through my papers.

"Are you not house-trained?" I hissed. "What do you mean by peeping into my private affairs like this?"

Then I noticed that she had been writing a message in the dust on the desktop. It said:

"THE KITCHEN ENTRANCE. TOMORROW NIGHT."

I looked her in the eyes. "Are you sure we have not met before?" I asked in a calm voice.

"Cover your eyes! Do not look at me!" pleaded Neferkitti. She was now in a panic, and trying not to stare at my collar.

I thought it was best to do as she asked. Padding up to the window I looked out towards the gate. The Spraetorians were playing mice again, by the look of it.

"Who wants to meet me the kitchen tomorrow night?" I asked. She said nothing. "Have no fear, for my collar cannot hear you."

"A friend of yours," she replied.

"Do not worry," I said "I will go to the kitchen tomorrow. But tell me, how do I know you?"

"My sister works at Spatopia. Her name is Cleocatra," she said.

"Of course," I said remembering that Cleocatra had a sister at the palace. "Please remember me to your sister." Then I began to tell her about the old days, when I was manager of Spatopia. Pleasant days! When I turned around I realised that she had been gone for some time.

As I rubbed away the message in the dust, I wondered if old friendships could disappear as easily. I thought of my old life at Spatopia. I wished that I could see my old friends again. Word has got about that I am the Emperor's Soothsayer as well a scribe with a loose tongue. I am shunned and hated by everyone, from Captain Matro to the rat catcher's servant. While I wear the collar, who wants a friend like me around?

The Official History of the Emperor Gattus Tiberius ('Catligula') as told to his scribe by the Best and Greatest one himself

The Emperor's words upon the occasion of the election of his pet, Rattus Rattus to the Senate were as follows:

"As I sit here on my cushion, a guest at the Senate on this happy day, I can see exactly what is wrong. It has long been said that the Senate is run by a pack of rats. This is not true. If rats were in charge at the Senate they would make a better job of it. They are resourceful creatures and would quickly sort out Rome's problems. The very first law they'd pass would get the drains running. It is for this reason that I have decided to

124

appoint my pet Rattus Rattus to the Senate. It has been whispered by some of the old fools that he is not fit for the job because he lacks experience in government. But he has all of the natural cunning of his fellow rats. He also has a true love of freedom, for he has gnawed his way out of his golden cage three times this week. Sometimes Imperial duties mean that I cannot go to the Senate. But you can be sure that my dear little Rattus will keep his one remaining yellow eye on the Senate when I am away. And he will have a yellow tooth ready to bite down upon the neck of any cat unwise enough to vote against my will. In grateful recognition, I have rewarded him with six servants to carry his golden cage, a silver sewage pipe to run in and as much rubbish as he can eat."

MAIUS III

May 3rd

The Dream Diary of Spartapuss, scribe to the Emperor - Part III

Last night I dreamed that I was floating in a little fishing boat. The seagulls cried as I cast my line into the mirror-smooth water.

In no time, I felt a bite. But the great fish I'd hooked was so strong that he pulled me out of the boat. As I tried to climb back into the boat, I saw a great wave coming. It was about to wash me and everything else away.

INTERPRETATION: Last night I dined late, taking advantage of an offer of three full bowls of fish liquor that the cooks were going to throw away. In the midst of my dream, just before the great wave overtook me, I woke up and went outside as I have been trained to do.

HADES' KITCHEN

The Spraetorian was late for my dream diary today and I began to fear that I'd miss the appointment that Neferkitti had taken so much trouble to arrange. Going as fast as I could without attracting unwanted attention, I went by the servants' route to the kitchen entrance. Catligula's new kitchen is built in the modern style in concrete and it is almost twice the size of the building it replaced. This is hard to believe, when you consider all the reports that under Catligula, our portions are getting smaller and smaller. As I stood at the entrance of this steamy underworld, the cooks were hissing orders to the porters, who were running about like headless chickens. I have always thought this expression a little unfair to chickens. If someone had chopped your head off with a blunt axe, would you walk calmly about the garden with a clear purpose? At any rate, I wondered how in Peus' name you could cook anything edible in this chaos. A half-hiss came from a space in between a tower of terracotta bowls and an enormous stack of mussel shells. Someone had eaten well this evening. I was marvelling at the streaks of perfect blue inside the shells when Tefnut's voice said:

"Stop staring and turn the other way at once!"

"I was not staring. I had no idea where you were hiding," I replied in an angry whisper. But I turned around obediently for I knew by now that there was no use disputing with a mystic. Without waiting for Tefnut to tell me that 'there is little time', I picked up the conversation where we had left it.

"I think I know where the Emperor is hiding the Moracle," I began. "In his private rooms he has a box marked with the sign of the white snake that swallows its tail, just like the ones in the Moracle cave."

"The Observer!" cried Tefnut excitedly. The mountain of mussel shells creaked.

"What?" I asked.

"Never mind. The Great White Snake is called the Observer. Go on, go on!" she said.

"There is something about this box with the sign of the snake on it. It smells familiar. I'm think the Moracle is inside," I explained.

Tefnut's voice was calm again.

"I will go there tonight. The Moracle must be freed.

If we do not meet again, remember that Catligula sees whatever you can see. If he takes the collar off, take any chance to get yours off too. Now leave me."

"Wait," I said. "You'll never get in there. He has guards on every door."

"Go now," she repeated.

"But the guards all know me. I can get you in!" I cried.

As I spoke these words, I realised that I wanted to help her more than anything. I was surprised when she agreed, with just one condition.

JOKERS AT THE DOOR

We picked our way through the kitchen towards the Emperor's apartments. It was slow progress. I had hardly taken a step before I smashed into a stack of bowls. I had a horror that we would be discovered but I need not have worried. There was a loud cheer from the pot washers. Such accidents are common in a kitchen.

"Tefnut!" I whispered. "Are you there?"

"Two steps away from you, always," came the reply.

Although I did not like to admit it, I was now less sure that her blindfold idea was going to work.

"Can't I take this off for a minute, I could walk ahead of you, off the lead?" I asked.

"This is the only way. We cannot risk the Emperor seeing us," she replied.

Two Spraetorians guard the servant's door that connects the kitchens to the Emperor's private apartments.

"Aye aye? What's up with His Little Pet?" said the first guard, seeing my blindfold.

"It hurts when I look at anything bright," I replied, lifting it up.

"It's all that peeping around," said the second guard. "I'd get yourself a proper job if I was you, before your eyes drop out."

"Or someone puts 'em out," added his friend.

"I'm prescribing him some herbs from the pharmacy," said Tefnut. "He'll be cured in a day or two, if he keeps them shut."

I padded casually forwards.

"Halt!" growled the first guard. "Where do you think you're going?"

I froze. What was I to do? I had convinced Tefnut that these guards knew me. We had not discussed what to do if they did not let us pass.

One Spraetorian hissed and shook his head. The other padded right up to me. He was a whisker away.

"Get that blindfold on properly!" he ordered. "Obey your doctor's orders. We can't have the Emperor's favourite going blind on us, can we?"

I nodded and did as I was told.

"On you go then doctor," said the other guard, waving us through the door.

Now we had another problem. The Imperial apartment was guarded by the Emperor's Purrmanian Bodyguards. No one is allowed in to see him unless they have been summoned, and their name is on the list. We could not crouch in the corridor all day. Tefnut suggested that we made our way to Catligula's rooms by means of the roof. Getting up there was the main problem. Every window we tried was locked, barred or nailed shut. Even if Tefnut could walk through iron bars, as I suspected she could, how could I follow? The food in the palace is rich, and I have always been too big boned for tight squeezes. Reluctantly, I pushed my nose through the bars into the night air.

"I'll never make it," I moaned.

"I will go alone," said Tefnut.

Outside, the night was warm. The stars were fiery dots but the night sky was light. Summer was coming early. When I leapt down from the window, defeated, the marble floor felt cool beneath my pads.

"Wait," I said. "If Fortune is willing, I know a better route."

Central heating has never been my passion. But as manager of Spatopia, Rome's finest Bath and Spa complex, I had to learn the secrets of the furnace. If the fire went out, the water went cold and the Spa's profits ran off down the waste drain. So when I noticed that the floor tiles here at the palace were cold to the touch, I knew it meant that the heating fires were not lit. With care, we might make our way to Catligula's apartments – by crawling underneath his floor.

On closer inspection, the floor was a great slab of concrete standing on many columns of bricks. This created a honeycomb underneath for the blessed warmth to circulate. With a little difficulty, Tefnut and I clawed our way in through the grate and began our long crawl. The air around us smelt smoky and the walls were soft to the touch – thick with the soot and the ash of ages. We were lost in a rabbit warren of tunnels. We crawled between the brick columns, more numerous than the statues on Paws Field. Tefnut led the way and I followed behind on the leash, blindfolded. I imagined this place when the great furnace was lit. I thought about the fiery world beneath our very paws as we walk about all day. For some reason this thought made me shiver.

DEAD WOOD BLOOMS

Our progress was slowed by mounds of half-burnt twigs and branches. They should have been raked out properly and not left to clog up the system.

"Those lazy rakers," I said. "Even here at the palace it is impossible to get good help."

Tefnut did not reply. Something guided her onward through the piles of ash and dust. At last we came to a spot where the ash was thickest underfoot. The walls of the tunnels and our ceiling – the underside of the Emperor's floor – were caked with thick soot.

"Are we close?" I asked. The old Emperor had liked his floor warm and the great furnace was next to the Imperial apartment.

"Listen," hissed Tefnut.

131

I heard faint voices.

"Waves?" hissed the unmistakable voice of Catligula.

Another voice replied. The last time I'd heard it, it had been inside my head.

"From the north seas, great waves will come bringing death, to your gates."

Despite its grim message, the high voice sounded matter-of-fact.

"Waves?" repeated Catligula, in horror.

"Great waves," said the Moracle wearily. She had a way of delivering dread prophecy as if she was reading a shopping list.

"Great waves, coming to wash me away!" hissed Catligula tragically.

To him, all the world was theatre, and the tragedy would be doubly bitter for anyone who dared to cross him.

"Tefnut!" I called, pulling at the leash to try to get her attention. But there was no answer. She must have dropped the lead. There was nothing for it. I slipped the blindfold off and searched the darkness, but she was gone.

I asked Fortune which way to crawl. She told me to the left, towards the furnace. I made my way quickly through the darkness, twisting past the half burnt wood and piles of ash. There was a scent coming from the far corner, a bitter perfume. Then came a pale light. As I moved towards it, I witnessed a transformation. The charred branches were sprouting fresh flowers. Green shoots rose from the ashes. Pale blooms were waving in the breeze, except there was no breeze. Pushing my way through the undergrowth, I saw Tefnut, far ahead of me. She seemed to be guiding the branches up and onwards. They began to crack up through the Emperor's floor.

In horror, I looked away. Remembering Tefnut's warnings about Catligula being able to see through my eyes, I scrambled to get my blindfold back on. I could not risk the Emperor seeing Tefnut. But how could I twist through this jungle and reach her, whilst wearing the blindfold? So I turned and retraced my steps through the maze of brick columns. It was a little easier without the blindfold but it took some minutes. Finally, I squeezed back out through the grate and brushed myself down. Then I padded purposefully on towards the Emperor's private chambers.

"Summoned again," I said to the big Purrmanian guarding the door.

He nodded and examined his list of names, but he did not find mine on it.

"Is there a problem?" I asked.

"You will wait behind the line while I check," he said politely.

"I think you'd better let me in," I replied firmly. "I was told the Emperor was having a terrible dream. He was calling out for me, personally."

The big Purrmanian looked unsure. From somewhere inside the apartments, there came a crash.

"Whenever he calls, we must answer!" I added.

"You can enter. I will check," said the bodyguard, waving me through the door.

BROKEN BISCUITS

I found the Emperor's stateroom, where he normally receives guests, in a terrible state. It was a dog's dinner. In fact it was worse than a dog's dinner, for no dog that I have known leaves its dinner half eaten or smears it over the walls. The floor was like a parrot's cage – the fine mosaic littered with half-eaten food and discarded toys and weapons. The mess was so great that I almost didn't notice the floor moving. Great branches were sprouting up, pushing the mosaic into bumps as they cracked through the floor. In the middle of all this, a thin grey cat was sniffing at the air. She stopped. She had seen me.

"Quiet!" hissed Tefnut.

I hadn't recognised her at first with her beautiful coat all covered in ashes and dust.

She sprang towards a side door that led into a bedroom. Like wary mice we crept through. Tefnut tasted the air for signs. Rather her than me – I thought. The air in the room was still and dead, every window had been nailed shut. On a low shelf next to the sofa was a wooden box, marked with the Great White Snake. It was a sign that grew no less unpleasant with repeated viewings.

"There!" I said, leaping to the box and struggling with the catch. In my excitement it slipped from my grasp and fell to the floor.

"Take care!" spat Tefnut in frustration. At last, I found the catch and opened the lid. My quest had led me to a biscuit-box that was completely empty save for a few stale crumbs. There was no sign of the Moracle.

I was in the middle of cursing the gods when Tefnut interrupted me.

"Sacred wafers," she said. "The food of the Moracle."

I picked a broken biscuit from the bottom of the box. It was dry and crumbly to the paw, and it gave off a powerful scent that took me back to the Moracle cave.

"Does the Moracle eat nothing but these?" I asked. "They look a bit dry to me."

Tefnut gave me a withering look.

"Well wise one, what else does she eat?" I asked.

"Seeds and nuts, or anything sweet. The food that mice eat," came the reply.

"So why these?" I asked – picking up a broken wafer and sniffing it. The smell was unusual, but not unpleasant when you got used to it. I had a nibble.

"Put that back!" hissed Tefnut. Only when I had replaced the broken wafer and closed the lid, would she explain.

"The Moracle eats them before she goes into the trance. To our kind, they are poison," she said.

"Urrrghh!" I cried – spitting the biscuit out and searching frantically for water to wash out my mouth. In a few moments, I had gone from hero to half-wit. Why had I been so sure that the Moracle was in the box?

FREE BLIND MOUSE

As I was making my apologies to Tefnut, an idea came into my head.

It wasn't long before I found what I was looking for. In the corner of the room, was a badly soiled rug with the design of a black rat feasting on a bowl of fruit. Lifting up this cover revealed a golden cage. The cage was filthier than the room it stood in. But it was well appointed. There was a golden wheel for exercise and the golden water bowl was studded with diamonds. The inscription on this bowl said: TO RATTUS RATTUS, FROM HIS DEAR DADDY.

Carefully, I opened the door. The cage had a sleeping chamber – another golden box, made in the style of a country villa. From inside, I heard a rustling. I lifted the roof off and found an enormous black rat and a white mouse, curled up together in the straw.

"Look," I whispered to Tefnut. "They're sleeping."

Just as these words left my mouth, the rat sprang up out of the box and sank its filthy yellow teeth into my nose.

I struggled to shake off my attacker. It is sometimes said that small things hurt the most. I prayed now that this was the case for it felt as if the rat's dagger-like teeth had torn my nose halfway off my face. At first it hurt so much that I could not cry out. Then the pain hit me once more and I let out a bitter howl.

"Guards! Guards!" called the rat in a voice that was more of a growl than a squeak. The alarm was raised.

"Leave now!" cried Tefnut.

Blood ran from the wound on my nose as I scrambled towards the door. I knew it was wrong, but I looked back once more at my friend only to see a huge form enter the room. The room trembled as Dogren of Purrmania shouted his challenge — something in the Purrmanian language that ended in spitting. Tefnut waited, her ash-covered coat pale against the marble.

"Ghost! Ghost!" called Rattus Rattus, turning circles in his cage.

"This is no ghost, I think," laughed Dogren, glaring at Tefnut. "I can see its feet."

Back in the Neuterberger Forest, each tribe had its own spirits who walked with the tribe. The tribes believed that their spirits have no feet, for they leave no prints behind.

"Get it! Get it!" squeaked the rat, in a voice so cruel it made me think that there is truth in the saying that pets take after their masters.

With frightening speed for such a big cat, Dogren lunged at Tefnut, aiming a bite that would have snapped her back in two like a chicken bone, if it had landed. Tefnut danced away in an automatic movement, as natural as the flick of a tail. Dogren smashed into the floor, sending pieces of mosaic flying. Taking her chance, Tefnut ran straight at her monstrous opponent, turning at the last moment and sliding between his legs. She could have been away and down the corridor, but Dogren now stood between her and the golden cage, where the Moracle sat watching.

Dogren spun around to face his pale challenger and hissed. He had defeated many opponents before. This one was quick, but she was flesh and blood. Feinting as if to strike again with his left paw he threw his whole body forward in an enormous spring. He had used this attack successfully many times before in the Arena. Small opponents could not believe a cat of his size could move so fast.

But Tefnut was not taken in. She was gone even before Dogren had finished thinking about the springing. He crashed to the floor and again the whole room shook. As the two opponents locked eyes, I alone had noticed that the golden cage had been knocked from its stand. The Moracle stepped gently out, darted across the floor and vanished through a crack in the tiles.

Dogren did not notice this. Twice he had attacked and twice his prey had evaded him. There would be no third escape. Now he waited, claws at the ready. But Tefnut did not attack. She started to dance in a stop-start rhythm. First moving forward and then seeming to fall, and then getting up again, in a strange little dance. Dogren had never seen anything like this before. Was it a victory dance? Did she think that he was defeated?

The air turned grey. A whirlwind drew ashes and cinders up from cracks in the floor. The room was so full of dust that I couldn't see my own whiskers.

"Run!" called Tefnut.

And with that I turned and ran from the room, blood from my nose dripping all over the marble.

MAIUS IV

May 4th

Bitten and Miserable

WHEN I WAS SUMMONED by Catligula today, I thought that my life was over. Surely by now, he'd know everything? My bitten nose, or Dogren's report would give me away. I spent a miserable night licking my wounds and dreaming of escape. But where could I run? There was nothing to do but report for scribing duty as commanded.

I entered the Imperial reception room to find Catligula unsteady on his paws, as if from a long night on the tiles. But apart from this he was normal, if that is possible. He said no word to me about the events of the day before. Instead, he commanded me to take out my pen, and write down this most unusual declaration.

The Official History of the Emperor Gattus Tiberius ('Catligula') as told to his scribe by the Best and Greatest one himself

As I sit here, paws on cushion, I look down on the faces of ordinary Romans going about their unimportant business. I am told that they are grateful to have an Emperor like me. They'd better be. Whilst the Senate are catnapping, their Emperor is wide-awake. I have found out about an enemy who plots against me. This watery menace will not speak his name out loud – for if he did it would only come out as bubbles. So I shall speak it for him. Neptuna, Lord of the Oceans – I defy you!

Romans – only this week I have learned that he plans to drown me under a great wave that he will summon up. This storm has been a long time brewing. Here are the proofs:

First – who puts grit into my mussels and makes my sea trout dinner taste all muddy?

Second – who orders rain every time I set a paw in my holiday villa on the beach at Pusstia?

And lastly, who sent the cruel storm that sank my shopping ship? That ship was carrying a precious cargo from Fleagypt – a golden water bottle, especially designed for Rattus Rattus, in the shape of a pyramid!

Neptuna – be afraid! I have this very day sent three legions to the seaside to dam this watery menace at the source. I will beat this barnacled bully. I will fight him on the beaches. I have instructed our generals to show no mercy. Our brave Scenturians have been ordered to do what they do best – all over the soft sand of our enemy, until he yields.

MAIUS V

May 5th

The Changing of the Bodyguard

DOGREN HAS PAID A HEAVY PRICE for losing the Moracle. He was lucky to get away with losing only his job as Head of the Purrmanian Bodyguards. I cannot be sure but I have heard a rumour that he has been posted to the kitchen. Chief of Pot Washers, as the Spraetorians are saying.

The Purrmanians were said to be climbing the walls when they heard the news. There was even talk of them going on strike or returning to Purrmania, although that threat is unlikely to amount to anything. They are too used to Rome's soft cushions and underfloor heating to head back to their forest homes – whatever their sad songs may say.

MAIUS VI

May 6th

Sick Note

IT IS WHISPERED that the Emperor is sick. His illness is unusual and rare. Captain Matro has summoned doctors from all over the Empire. But he was not too sick to summon me for some scribing

> The Official History of the Emperor Gattus Tiberius ('Catligula') as told to his scribe by the Best and Greatest one himself

> Friends, Romans, urrrgh! As I lie here in my sick bed I want you to know that if that sea-weeded fool Neptuna thinks that he has the upper paw, he is very much mistaken. I will show him what happens when an Emperor's fur is rubbed up the wrong way. I will ram his slimy beard down his plug-hole, 'til he chokes on his own salt spray. Urrgh! My doctors have told me that I must not become over excited or I may die. They say that I am

too sick to do battle, so the war must wait for a while. Many of you have decided to stand outside the palace gates and pray for my recovery. Make sure you pray harder. And for Peus' sake, pray quietly! I hear everything!

MAIUS VII

May 7th

The Sound of the Crowd

A SIZEABLE CROWD has gathered outside the palace gates to pray for the Emperor's recovery. The citizens are waving signs that read: 'Star – Shine Forever!' and 'Mewpiter take me instead of Him!' When the Spraetorians went out to order them to be quiet, they started to riot.

A second entry in my diary today. At last the news that I have been waiting for. Another message, written in the dust on my desk asks me to be in the kitchen tomorrow.

MAIUS VIII

May 8th

Chief Cook

IT IS RARE THING when a palace rumour turns out to be true, but today I have seen it with my own eyes, if only for a brief moment before putting my blindfold on. I arrived in the kitchen shortly after dinnertime and I found the place transformed. Gone were the stacks of dirty bowls and old scratching posts. Everything was in its proper place. The floor was spotless. The porters and cooks padded briskly but carefully from place to place. And there was no talking, except for answers to the chef's questions. I was worried that I'd chosen a bad place for the meeting, because everyone seemed to know exactly what they were doing. It is easier to blend into chaos than order. I heard a clear voice singing:

> 'How we miss old Mother Forest,
> And our Neuterberger homes,
> For they dragged us from our forest,
> And they brought us here to Rome,
>
> Though we fought them in Klaws' Garden,
> Over every leaf and tree,
> Still they licked us and they tricked us,
> And they took our territory.'

The whispers were true. Catligula had transferred the Purrmanian Bodyguards to kitchen duty. They'd certainly got the kitchen running smoothly. I'd never seen the place so clean. I was still taking this in when a whisper from behind a tower of drinking bowls told me to follow. When my eyes were safely covered, we padded down to the back of the kitchen, where a side door led into the dairy.

When I was satisfied that no one had followed us I asked Tefnut if the Moracle was safe. In a weary voice, she replied that in truth, she did not know.

"Didn't you find her?" I asked.

"Yes, of course," she replied. For the first time since we'd met, her voice sounded old and weary.

"There were certain complications," she said. "It seems that the Moracle does not want to be rescued. It seems that she is enjoying her freedom."

This was the last thing I expected to hear. Captured, yes, dead even, but not wanting to come back? Outside in the kitchen, the Purrmanians had stopped singing.

"Don't worry," I said confidently, "she'll come back when she's ready."

"I am not worried" Tefnut replied. But her voice, usually such a reliable servant, kept giving her away. I felt her tail flick as she sighed.

"Spartapuss, I must ask you about what happened back in the Moracle cave. Have you told me everything?"

"Yes," I replied.

"Are you sure? Is there anything else?" she pressed.

I had no clue what she was talking about.

"Uncover your eyes and look at the floor," she ordered.

In the sandy floor she'd drawn a picture of a snake, eating its own tail. I swallowed hard. It was a relief to get the blindfold on again so that I did not have to meet her eyes.

"The Scenturian told me to leave the Moracle cave and report to the palace. I suppose I was trying to follow the guards. But I took a wrong turning."

"Go on," said Tefnut.

"I went down a tunnel that ran under the hill. There was a city of villas for the dead. Actually, some of them looked nice. Good enough for the living..."

"That is all?" asked Tefnut.

"Yes," I lied.

"No," said Tefnut. She pulled the blindfold down from my eyes and stared at me, not with anger but with a powerful gaze. But I could not meet her eyes. I choked instead.

"Look away!" I cried. "Remember the collar. Catligula will see you."

Tefnut ignored me. Apparently, the time for secrets was over.

I told her about the birds and how I had escaped from the Great White Snake. "I am sorry. I meant to tell you," I sighed.

"You are ashamed that you ran from the Observer. There is no shame in that. But to hold back information from me. For that, there can be no excuse."

I nodded.

"The Observer is old and powerful. He is slow but he is certain as the grave. Nothing in this world can stop him. Where the Moracle goes, the Observer must follow." "'Where one goes the other must follow', that has a familiar sound to it," I thought.

"So he'll follow the Moracle to the palace then?" I asked. She nodded saying

"He will go by the shortest path."

"What can we do?" I asked.

"Nothing," she replied. "You have done enough."

I do not like silence, and when a space in the conversation appears I like to fill it. But for once I kept my mouth shut. Tefnut left without another word.

In the next room another old song boomed out. It was a song about the forest, about victory in battle. The words were sad beyond measure but the tune was cheerful. I wondered if it was worth the bother. If the old country far away was so great, why did they leave it in the first place? And at least they have homes here in Rome to go back to on leave.

MEWNONIUS I

June 1st

The Waiting Room

THESE LAST TWO WEEKS have been the most hopeless that I can remember. I have been no stranger to ill fortune before, but this time I have brought my troubles upon my own head. The Moracle is still missing. There has been no news about the Observer. I cannot see my old friends for fear of what this wretched collar might reveal. Mogullania has banned me from Spatopia. Captain Matro has ordered me not to speak to him. I have heard nothing from Tefnut since she walked away. Last night I was considering alternative careers. It is said that they are in need of settlers for a marshy outpost on the frontier with Catage. I would apply but I cannot stand mosquitoes. I have a horror of being bitten on the pads.

MEWNONIUS II

June 2nd

Grass and Warm Water

CAPTAIN MATRO has given the Spraetorians orders to arrest anyone bringing the Emperor food. He is allowed to eat nothing but grass and warm water. It seems to be working, for he is less troubled by dreams and he has just summoned me. He has need of a scribe again.

> The Official History of the Emperor Gattus Tiberius ('Catligula') as told to his scribe by the Best and Greatest one himself

> Romans, for the past few weeks you have asked only one question. How is our dear Emperor? When will He be well again? Is He still off His food? My scribe has just told me that that is three questions, but we gods do not count like you mortals. The answer is that I am feeling MUCH BETTER. Although of course, I now have no need of food like the rest of you, water has never tasted sweeter from the bowl. Biscuits have never tasted better from the box!

Now for news about the War with Neptuna, may barnacles gnaw at his gnarly nose! The doctors say that I am too ill to travel, so I am sending someone in my place to do my business on his beaches. I am told that Dogren of Purrmania has done a good job in the kitchen recently. So I'm sending a cook instead of a general. The other Gods will be impressed when my chef stews the senses out of that seaweed-bearded bully.

P.S. It has come to my attention that during my illness, many of you asked the gods to take your lives in exchange for mine. Now that I am recovered, please kill yourselves promptly. A promise is a promise.

MEWNONIUS III

June 3rd

Good God

CATLIGULA'S CHANGE from Emperor to God seems to be going very well. Happiness has broken out all over the city. He has never been more popular. No one at the Senate has dared to ask questions. Of course, the Emperor Augustpuss was made a god after his death. But that was mainly to keep the barbarians happy. Their temples were full of golden bulls or mysterious birds so it seemed like a good idea to give them a decent Roman feline to worship.

Apart from myself, the unhappiest Roman of them all is Captain Matro. I have never seen such sour looks. It may be the strain of attending to a god every day. They can be very demanding. Or perhaps he is jealous that Dogren and the Purrmanians have been sent to the beach to win easy honours doing battle with the sea?

MEWNONIUS IV

June 4th

On the List

ILL NEWS FROM NEFERKITTI, the cleaner. Her father is on the list of those who promised the gods that they would fight in the Games if Catligula recovered from his illness. I had to ask the obvious question – why would anyone make so stupid a promise? Apparently he was out with a party of friends from work and they all did it together. Poor Neferkitti. She came to me because I am known to have some influence with the Emperor. So I have decided to do whatever I can to save her father from the Games. I have decided to ask Captain Matro for his help. I know that the Captain and I have not understood each other in the past. But I will go and reason with him.

MEWNONIUS VI

June 6th

The Watchword

AGAINST MY BETTER JUDGEMENT, I found myself outside Captain Matro's room. The Captain was not alone, judging by the scent in the air.

Putting on my blindfold, I pushed my nose through the door.

"You!" said a familiar voice. There was a nasty base note to Mogullania's perfume. "Listening at doors again?" she hissed.

The whiskers on my right side gave a twinge.

"Captain. You can see that I am blindfolded. Aren't you wondering why a spy would enter a room blindfolded?"

"Because he's a half-wit?" said Mogullania. By the general laughter I knew that we three were not alone in the room. The Captain was curious and he let me speak. I explained about the business of the collar and how Catligula could see what I see. Then I told him about Neferkitti's father being on the list for the Games and asked for his help.

"An interesting roll of the dice," said Mogullania, who secretly liked to gamble although she would never allow Clawdius to do so.

Captain Matro began a speech. It was as if he had rehearsed it many times before, in his mind.

"Spartapuss, you came here blindfolded. Well, we have all been blind my friend, blind to the evil in our midst. I am just an honest soldier and it is the soldier's way to follow orders. But our Emperor is mad. He makes war on the sea, he appoints a rat to the Senate. Where will his sickness lead us? Some of us must act for the common good and stop him. We must rid Rome of this tyrant and all of his line. What choice have we, but to act quickly, before the noose closes around our own necks."

Stirred onwards by his own words, Matro's voice rose to a crescendo. But now he lowered it. He was contemplating a terrible deed that would mean breaking the oath of loyalty that he had taken.

"For the greater good of Rome," said Matro, "it is up to us to put the Emperor out of his misery."

"How must we act?" asked a voice from the corner.

"For Peus' sake, how do you think?" hissed Mogullania.

"Yes. But what's the best way to get the job done? Poison?" asked another voice. "There is no time for poison," hissed Mogullania. "Besides, the Emperor eats nothing but biscuits these days."

"It must be a quick kill," said the Captain. "We will strike tomorrow."

They planned to assassinate Catligula at the Games given in honour of his recovery. The strongest opposition would come from the Emperor's Purrmanian

Bodyguards. But Matro was sure that we could break through the Purrmanian lines to the Emperor. He himself would strike the killer blow.

When someone questioned whether Matro's Spraetorians would join in the attack, the Captain sprang to his troops' defence.

"My Spraetorians are loyal. They would follow me through the Land of the Dead in a heartbeat," he said.

Mogullania yawned. Matro had such a romantic view of his soldiers and their belief in his leadership.

"Matro my dearest, don't you think it might be better to distract the Purrmanians and get the Emperor on his own?" she said sweetly.

It's not quite as easy as that dearest," said Matro patiently. "This has to be a carefully-planned military operation."

I had a bad feeling about where this was leading. And I was right.

"Spartapuss is well known to the guards," said Mogullania.

I felt a fatherly paw on my shoulder. "Spartapuss," purred Captain Matro.

"Will you do this for Rome?"

I remembered the Games of Purrcury. Catligula had been trapped under the wreckage of his crashed chariot. And I pulled him out, because I could not stand and watch another creature suffer. But how many lives had been taken because of my compassionate act? Would it have been better to have left him there, to die? I thought of the vision I'd seen in the Moracle cave. Then I remembered Neferkitti's father and the others forced to take their own lives or to fight in the Games because of the Emperor's madness. Catligula had not wronged me personally. He had been a better friend to me than Clawdius. But tomorrow, I would betray him.

When I gave Captain Matro my answer, he was delighted.

"You will do right for Rome, Spartapuss. She will not forget it."

"How will we know when to strike?" I asked.

"Wait for the watchword 'Repurrblic'" said Matro. "And when you hear the shout, strike without mercy."

MEWNONIUS VII

June 7th

This is The End

THIS WILL SURELY be the last entry of my diary. I am trying to think about a positive result tomorrow. But I do not rate our chances highly, and if it goes ill, we will surely be put to death.

Slaves who try to kill their masters are sewn up into a bag of rats and thrown into the river Tiber. But Catligula will surely come up with something worse than this for us. At any rate I shall be soon be free of this accursed collar.

I wish now that I could see my friends one last time.

Tefnut – I am sorry for not telling you the whole truth.

Neferkitti – I am sorry about your father.

Clawdius – whatever ill will there was between us, I am free of it now. I am a freedcat after all.

I have decided to burn this diary - for it may reveal too much if it is found.

I have decided not to burn this diary, for the burning may draw the attention of the Purrmanians. I shall throw it into a ditch on the way to the Games tomorrow.

It seems a shame to leave this page unfilled but there is nothing else to say so I shall finish this with the words of the philosopher Pawralius, which we had on a poster at the Spa.

'Soon, very soon, we will be ashes, or a skeleton, and a name. Or not even a name. And so above all things remember this...'

For Peus' sake. I cannot now remember the rest of it

MEWNONIUS XXVII

June 26th

A Stain on my Record

WRITING CAN BE AN UNPLEASANT BUSINESS. There is a reek of fish and sewage coming from this diary because I threw it into a drainage ditch by the market. Fortune willed it that I should recover it, a little stained but intact. I shall continue my story. Where I last left off, I had joined the plot against Catligula. But plotters have a habit of not telling the whole truth. And so it was to be.

OFFICIAL PROGRAMME

Games – in honour of the Emperor's recovery

I.   Opening Ceremony (music: slow and fast)
II. The Parade of the Gladiators.
III. Distribution of fish and cold cream.
IV. A theatrical event in honour of The Emperor's victory against the Sea God Neptuna.
V.   Lunchtime feasting and executions.
VI. The Games continue.
VII. Closing ceremony.

These Games are brought to you in association with Bathhausia, Rome's finest Purrmanian-style Bath House.

Note to our customers: the algae problem in the plunge pool has been dealt with.

OUTSIDE THE BOX

As the band tuned their instruments, we stood on the platform outside the Imperial Box. Clawdius, Mogullania and I. Clawdius, famous for his short paws and long pockets, was paying for the Games – at Mogullania's request.

Matro, who was in charge of the arrangements, had asked the Emperor if, on such an important occasion, he would have need of his trusted scribe to record his historic words. So I was to watch the Games from the Imperial Box. I had been provided with a purple pass to get in. And today there was to be an extra death on the programme.

Our plan was simple. We were to wait until the parade of Gladiators was under way. The Emperor would make his way to the Imperial Box to take to his cushion, fashionably late as usual. His Purrmanian Bodyguards would be at his side. After he had entered the Imperial box, I was to approach with a message, saying that the new Fleagyptian Governor had just arrived with a marvellous present for his pet Rattus.

I would then lead Catligula down the passage towards the backstage area and Matro's Spraetorians would get between the Emperor and his Bodyguards. On hearing the cry, 'Repurrblic!' Matro's loyal Spraetorians would do the rest.

It was the custom that none could enter the Imperial Box until the Emperor himself had taken to his cushion. Clawdius circled nervously, dragging his back paws as usual. Mogullania hissed at him under her breath. He was so unfeline, especially on occasions of state when they were together in public.

"Stand still why don't you!" she hissed.

Clawdius said nothing but stopped circling. He exchanged few words with Mogullania these days, and none of them were pleasant. Why had she been so keen to marry him? Apart from his position as a member of the Imperial Family, and his great personal wealth of course. Any genuine affection between them had been strangled at birth. Clawdius gave his wife a little smile and unwrapped a scroll. Did he know about the plot?

"For Peus' sake, stop shuffling around and sit still," hissed Mogullania again.

Surely Clawdius was not in on it. Although it was said in the Spa that he had once got into trouble with his tutors for asking too many questions about the old days of The Repurrblic, when the Senate had ruled instead of the Emperor.

"I am not sh-shuffling," said Clawdius, looking hurt. Small trickles of foam formed around his mouth.

Mogullania turned away, disgusted.

"I am m-making some changes to my speech. I wish Purrmanipuss were here. He would have loved these Games."

I remembered how much Clawdius loved Purrmanipuss. Everyone loved Purrmanipuss. He had been a fearless soldier, a confident speaker, a loyal brother.

Mogullania took the scroll from Clawdius.

"Captain Matro spent a lot of time writing that speech for you. We don't want you rambling on and ruining it." Cold as the tomb, she passed me the scroll.

"See that he does not have it back before it is time for him to speak," she ordered. Then dropping her voice to the lowest of whispers she said:

"Make sure he stays at the Emperor's side at all times."

At that moment I knew what was in her heart. So much for the good of Rome. Our blow for freedom would not stop at the Emperor. His uncle Clawdius was also marked for death this day. Mogullania would soon be free to spend her husband's fortune, without having to look at his dribbling face every day. This was an unexpected spin. Perhaps Catligula deserved death. He himself had ordered the death of the old Emperor. Clawdius however, had many faults, but were any of them so great that I could be his judge and executioner?

"You can rely on me," I replied.

As I spoke, I remembered the words of the philosopher Pawralious, from the poster.

'Say no evil,

Think no evil,

Do no evil.

That is all.'

And I wondered if what I was about to do, was good or evil.

THE MARCH OF THE GLADIATORS

At that moment, there was a blast on the tuba. I have never liked the tuba. It was the signal for the start of the parade of the Gladiators. Catligula was late as usual, but that was of no importance, for the Games proper could not start without him. On occasions such as these he would often spend hours at his mirror, practising his fierce expressions and gestures: claws out for death, claws in and the fallen would live to die another day.

The band struck up with the March of the Gladiators, an over dramatic piece of music, far too slow for marching. Although our platform was shaded, the sun showed the Gladiators no mercy as they began their warm-up. They paraded around the ring in their teams. The yellows looked worried. The red Pumillo looked strong. The Furasians in their pea green looked confident. This was no surprise – everyone knew that Catligula favoured the pea greens.

From my place on the platform outside the Imperial Box, it was a long drop to the sand on the arena floor. I searched the faces of the Gladiators. From where I sat they looked liked tiny ants, running around in circles as they went through their fighting drills. Who cares if an ant lives or dies? Not another ant – that is as sure as sunrise. Somewhere among their ranks was Neferkitti's father. I wondered if he would fight with the sword or with the net and trident. I thought of my last appearance in the Arena, when I had been the entertainment. I might be on the bill again if Captain Matro's plot failed and I was unmasked as a conspirator. As the saying goes, 'There is always room for another execution at lunchtime', or perhaps Catligula would have all of us thrown to the wild beasts. And even if the plot succeeded, it was no guarantee of safety. When an Emperor is murdered, it is not unknown for his Bodyguards to go wild, taking their revenge against innocent and guilty alike.

CHICKENS TO THE SLAUGHTER

Noises on the steps shook me from these thoughts. There was no mistaking the stomp of the ironclad paws of the Purrmanian Bodyguards. The Emperor had arrived. The band struck up with a tuba-heavy tune called 'Caesar is it Life or Death?' This has never been popular with the Gladiators, for the chorus is 'Death! Death! Death!'

The Emperor padded up the stairs, as calm as a sacred chicken on a sacrifice day. As he walked past, Catligula began to roll his eyes and shuffle in a cruelly accurate imitation of Clawdius. Clawdius capered about, as if he too was in on the joke. Mogullania cringed. On occasions like this she would gnaw one of her own limbs off to escape from her husband.

When the guests of honour had taken in their places it was time for the servants to enter. I pushed up to the front of the line.

I felt Mogullania's eyes on me. The time for me to play my part had come. I must lead Catligula into the trap. Approaching the Emperor with my body low to the ground, I said my piece. He held my gaze as I spoke. My paw went to the 'witches' collar' around my neck. The two collars were so close now that they were almost touching. Did he know that I was lying? Then he sprang from his cushion. The Purrmanian Bodyguards, who had been watching the Gladiators warming up, were caught by surprise. With a bound, the Emperor flew down the wooden stairs with myself and the Purrmanians following behind him.

STAGE FRIGHT

Captain Matro and his guards were waiting in the alley, filing their claws and fingering their blades. Matro was already running over his speech in his mind. When the hour came, every Roman must be like a tiger, ready to strike a blow for freedom against the dictator. In a few paces, the dictator would be within striking range.

But Catligula never turned down that alley. He took the backstage door and stalked straight on at a great pace. Somewhere behind me, I heard a cry:

"Repurrblic? Repurrblic?" It was shouted as a question rather than a statement.

When we reached the area where the actors were warming up, Catligula called me forward.

"Cancelled, you say?" he said in amazement.

"Yes Caesar," I replied. "They're saying there is no star among them bright enough to play the role."

Now I was acting. The play to be given in Catligula's honour was going to be a dramatic re-enactment of Catligula's battle with Neptuna, Lord of the Oceans. I had led Catligula backstage with the story that the play had been cancelled, for there was no actor in Rome good enough to play the part of Catligula in the show.

But there was one problem – the actors knew nothing about my plan. Thinking fast, I led Catligula towards a door with a golden star on it. Inside the dressing room, two well-trained voices were swapping stories.

"The Squeaks? Blast their markings! They are the worst payers in the business!" cried Purroo, adding some more barnacles to his sea-weedy beard.

"They invented the theatre – and now they think they own it," he continued.

"When a player goes touring at my stage in life, he needs a single basket room or nothing."

"Well I hope you told them where they could put

it," said Mniaow, waving his golden thunderbolt to illustrate his point.

I decided that I needed to create an entrance.

"The Emperor approaches!" I cried, crashing in through the door with Catligula and his Bodyguards behind me.

Mniaow and Purroo were taken completely by surprise. At first they thought it was a joke but the sight of the Purrmanians armed to the teeth soon straightened their crooked smiles.

"Get down on the ground! You are in the presence of your Emperor. Your God walks among you!" I cried, with a sweeping gesture, which I hoped they'd appreciate. It was very much in the classical style. The actors stared up at their Emperor like starstruck kittens. Catligula pinched Purroo hard on the ear.

"They are right!" exclaimed Catligula in horror.

"This creature could never do me justice. And I don't have a beard."

"Caesar, I think that he is supposed to play the sea God Neptuna," I said.

"You mean this… this little runt was cast to play the role of me?" spat the Emperor.

"Yes Caesar. Unless, for the sake of art, you could step in?" I suggested.

"For the sake of art I must!" cried Catligula.

"On your feet Neptuna. Now, where are my lines?"

Mniaow, in complete shock, passed the Emperor his script.

Then he made the biggest mistake of his career.

"Might I know if Caesar requires any help with the stage directions?" he asked politely.

Catligula stopped dead.

"Insolence?" he spat. "Throw him to the beasts. They are marvellous directors. They'll draw a good performance out of him," he ordered.

Stunned, poor Mniaow began to tremble.

"Mercy!" he sobbed theatrically.

"What? Oh very well," said Catligula.

"As an act of mercy, you may watch my performance, before you die."

I had come to these Games to save Rome and Neferkitti's father. Then I had changed my mind and decided to save Clawdius from Captain Matro and his own wife. But my latest plan had just condemned an innocent actor to an excruciating death. I had to save him, but I could only save them one at a time!

"Caesar Best and Greatest," I began. "I beg to leave your side and return to Clawdius. He's forgotten his speech."

Catligula nodded. But when I did not leave immediately, he looked up from his script.

"Yes? What is it?" he asked.

"Great Caesar, be merciful. Make a change to the running order!" I begged.

"Why?" asked Catligula, pawing through his script with a scowl.

"The play is scheduled to go on after the Gladiators.

But think of your audience. When word gets round that you are appear in person, I fear that the crowd may go wild, with the anticipation."

"I suppose you are right," said Catligula. "Tell Clawdius I'm going on first!"

"Caesar, can I borrow this actor?" I asked, pointing at Mniaow. "For Clawdius has never been Rome's most comfortable public speaker."

"V-v-v-very well." said Catligula. His Clawdius impression was good. But the room was silent until I began to laugh. He acknowledged the joke with a wave of his paw and ordered two Bodyguards to accompany Mniaow and me back to the Imperial Box. They had instructions to throw Mniaow to the wild beasts as soon as the play was over.

THE CALLING

As we approached the Imperial Box, the last Gladiators were leaving the ring. The warm up was over. Cha-ron, Lord of the Underworld and Purrcury, God of Thieves and Gladiators, were trying to entertain the crowd. But the mob was restless and began a slow clap. Cha-ron spat and waved his long hook at them, his task was to drag the bodies of the fallen through the Gate of Death. But not before his friend Purrcury had given them a poke with his red hot iron to check that there was nothing funny going on. It was not unknown for a Gladiator to try to fake death in order to survive the Games.

From the front row I heard a cry:

"Those who are about to die, get on with it!"

Cha-ron tried to grab the offender with his hook, without success.

When we'd got to the top of the stairs my heart sank. Clawdius was nowhere to be seen. I had hoped to keep him safe, with the Purrmanians to protect him. There was no sign of Mogullania either. There was nothing to do but start the Games. So I stood in Clawdius' place whilst Mniaow, carrying on like a true professional, stood on a box and shouted my lines to the crowd.

"Friends, Romans, foreigners. Welcome to the Games given in honour of the recovery of your Emperor and God, Gattus Tiberius..."

"Catligula! Catligula" shouted a voice in the crowd. This drew a huge cheer whilst the guards, both Purrmanians and Spraetorians furiously searched the front rows for the offender. The Emperor hated his nickname and it was death to speak it in public, if they could catch you.

"Later..." I continued. "Later we will bring you battle, lunch and executions."

There were cheers and excited yowls from the mob.

"But first we have some special entertainment of a theatrical nature."

There were hisses and shouts of "No! Shame!"

"I give you your own dear Emperor, in the role of himself."

Silence.

"In a new play that he has written himself, called 'The War of the Waves'."

THE PLAY

The carpenters and slaves pulled on a hundred ropes, and a great blue cloth was hauled across the floor of the Arena.

I heard a cry from below the platform. Was someone calling my name? The slaves and carpenters pulled harder, encouraged by the whips of the stage manager. I looked out from the platform to see where the shout had come from. There was a blast on the tuba and two great islands moved slowly into position. In the crowd below me, every pair of eyes was on the spectacle. Only I was looking at a figure struggling up through the crowd in my direction. It was Neferkitti.

At that moment, one of the islands trod on a carpenter and let out a wild trumpeting sound. The mob roared their approval.

In the middle of the ring, in a barge, stood Catligula with a thunderbolt in one paw and a script in the other.

"Oi, Neptuna! Where's your water?" shouted a joker in the crowd.

Catligula scowled, dismissed the interruption with a wave of the paw. Then, he roared:

'Oh water God,
Let loose your flood,
Into your brother's great big tub!'

Nothing happened. So Catligula cried:
'I, Gaius the God command it!'

And on that cue water began to flood into the Arena from hundreds of hidden pipes. It rushed in with such force that within half a minute, the whole floor was flooded. Catligula's barge bobbed majestically on the waves.

The crowd gasped. They had never seen anything like this before. They weren't sure about the lines, but they had to admit that the special effects were good.

By now, Neferkitti had got as close as she could to me. She'd reached a position underneath the platform. She was shouting something but her voice was lost in the sound of the rushing water.

Now that he had the crowd's attention, Catligula began:

'There's water, water everywhere!
As far as the eye can see,
But don't you know,
We gods don't row,
So I'll need a tow,
To pull me across the sea.'

In a section of the crowd there was uproar. Catligula's verses had rhymes in them! Rhymes were unacceptable in classical poetry and bad rhymes doubly so. But their shouts of hate were stopped in their mouths when a great elephant, who had been kneeling down half submerged, rose perfectly on cue. The elephant had been decorated with all the skill of the make-up artists to look like a sea monster. It didn't like being a sea monster, which is why it had trod on the carpenter earlier when he poked it with a spear. But its friend, who had done this sort of thing before, gave it a reassuring trumpet. Together, they tugged on the great ropes and Catligula's barge began to glide majestically across the Arena. The audience cheered and applauded wildly. This was rather good.

Mniaow and I both let out deep sighs. I had no clue what Neferkitti was trying to say. Mniaow was sighing at the applause, which should have been for him. The Emperor had stolen it.

At this moment a little circular boat floated into the middle of the Arena. In it stood the actor Purroo wearing the traditional costume of the sea god Neptuna, a trident and a beard. He had a script too – for Catligula had made some last-minute changes. They were supposed to have had one elephant each for a start, but the Emperor had taken both of them. His boat turned in circles as he got ready to say his new lines. It was a good job he was classically trained. He gave them his best delivery.

'I am Neptuna,
Lord of the Seas.
It's nice underwater,
Away from the fleas.
I rule the oceans,
By night and by day.
So ask my permission,
Before sailing my way.'

Catligula scowled his fiercest scowl.

'Enough of your spouting,
You bloated old cod,
I don't need your permission,
For I am your God!'

And he pointed his thunderbolt at Neptuna – who cowered at the bottom of his boat. There was a roll of thunder, provided by a group of Spraetorians wobbling their shields and a crack of lightning from a firecracker.

The sea, which had been glass-smooth, now began to roll and ripple. With a crack of the whip, the stage manager had turned the wave machine on.

Neferkitti was now pointing frantically at one of the islands in middle of the flooded Arena.

One of Catligula's moving 'islands' reared up and gave a mighty trumpet. Floating past it, on the hub of a broken chariot wheel, was a small white mouse.

The elephant gave out a bellow of terror and charged leftwards, creating a mighty wave that sent Neptuna's boat spinning in wild circles. The elephant had not been trained for water, and nothing could prepare him for this. He could not stand mice. They have quivering bodies and little pink feet that could have been scurrying around anywhere. Now one was floating up to him at trunk level.

He trumpeted hard and charged at the nearest side of the Arena. But he was tied to Catligula's barge by a rope.

The ruler of the Feline Empire was thrown violently towards the side of his barge. He scrabbled at the edge of the boat, his back paws kicking at the thin air. Then with a wobble, he plunged into the water.

But this God was a poor swimmer. He started to thrash about and cry out. Was this the end? Would history lose its greatest actor to a chance boating accident? It was not to be. His paw struck something solid. Clinging onto the chariot wheel, he looked straight into the eyes of The Moracle.

"You!" he cried bitterly. "Is it my destiny to die here?"

"Destiny, destiny, that's all they're ever interested in," thought the Moracle.

Catligula clung on with his front paws, almost losing hold as another great wave sent him rising up. He gazed at the Moracle in amazement.

"I can read your thoughts! It is happening. I am becoming a God."

At last, the pressure sent the waves bursting over the sides, drenching the front rows of the crowd in muddy water.

"Cease cruel waves! Obey me! I, your God command it!" cried Catligula, who had grabbed his thunderbolt as it floated past and was now trying to wave it.

"Oh dear," thought the Moracle. But he wasn't thinking about Catligula's performance.

For the waters had began to bubble like rabbit stew left to boil dry. In the centre of the Arena, a muddy whirlpool was forming.

The crowd loved this effect. It was by far the most spectacular of the day.

The water was pulled clockwise in a screw, twisting into the Arena floor. Catligula and the Moracle were being sucked towards its centre.

"I do not know my own power!" said Catligula. "Waves – hear me now. Stop!" he commanded.

BLIND GOD IN THE RING

The crowd gasped again. From the centre of the whirlpool, came the head of a Great White Snake. The mob thought this latest effect was stunning.

"You have to admire Catligula's theatrical vision," said Mniaow with the hint of a tear in his eye. "If only he would drop the poetry, his plays would be triumphs."

Only I knew that what Tefnut had feared had come to pass. Here was the Observer, that I had last seen in the dead city underneath the cave of the Moracle.

I have never liked snakes. And I have a particular dislike of sea snakes – for under the waves you cannot see what they are up to. In this case it was obvious. It was making its way towards the chariot wheel.

"Not again," thought the Moracle.

For the third time in his life, Catligula was afraid. Long ago, when he was a kitten he was butted by a goat in the palace gardens. That goat had paid the ultimate price. Catligula had its horns sawn off and made into a scratching post. The second time he'd felt fear had been at the Games of Purrcury, when he had been trapped under a crashed chariot. Then he had feared that nobody would come to his aid. But this fear was different. The Great Snake towered over everything. It was taller even than the rebuilt statue of the Emperor Tiberius. He tried to stare it out but it looked straight through him.

He seized the Moracle in his paw.

"This little witch is what you're here for," hissed Catligula.

"Well she is mine, monster, so you must do my bidding!"

It was useless. The Observer could not hear. Long ages ago his ears had shrivelled away and been shed. He found his way by vibrations and taste. And something always drew him towards the Moracle. He was nearly there now.

The water was almost gone. Catligula stood in the

mud. The crowd cheered and hissed in equal parts, hoping for a good special effect for the main course and then some proper Gladiator fighting for afters. I heard a voice from one of the front rows cry:

"Repurrblic!"

Seizing his chance, Captain Matro had got into the Arena, with a small group of Spraetorians.

"Repurrblic, Repurrblic" they called to their fellows. It was the signal for Catligula's assassination. The crowd didn't know it, but murder was now back on the programme. More Spraetorians sprang their Captain's aid.

The mob cheered. The guards were going to help the Emperor with that snake. They wondered if it would bleed red blood or spout green slime when they hacked into it with their swords.

"Spartapuss!" called a voice above me in the female seating. Neferkitti had made her way through the crowds to a position above the Imperial Box. She was screaming for me to help the Moracle.

ON THE ROOF

It was a giant's leap from the Imperial Box down to the Arena floor – and I have never been a great leaper. As I sprung onto the rail, I looked down through the cheaper seating towards the floor of the Arena, far below. There was little chance of surviving such a leap. But I had to try. I made ready to spring.

"No! Wait!" cried Neferkitti.

"Shut up Fleagyptian – let him do it!" shouted a fat tabby, who had been complaining loudly about the ridiculous amounts that Gladiators get paid for the amount of actual fighting they do.

"Jump! Jump!" cried his friend. They'd come for blood and they'd had no sniff of it so far, only theatre. But I was not about to give them what they wanted.

"Not that way. Take the roof!" shouted Neferkitti. She pointed at the canvas sunshade that was suspended over the good seats by the Imperial Box. It was retracted now, for they usually brought it out when the sun was hottest during the midday executions. I climbed up from the platform and caught hold of it. I called to Mniaow, who was mouthing something. His last words perhaps?

"Mniaow! Lower the roof," I called. The actor played his part.

The roof unfolded, swinging me out into the centre of the ring. It was a long drop to the mud below me, some fifty tails down by the look of it. The Arena was now full of Spraetorians, all running towards

Catligula, with death in their eyes. But the Emperor had no clue about Matro's plot. When he saw the guards running to his aid, he was pleased. For every great actor needs a cast of little spear carriers to make their greatness stand out.

Turning his back on the monster, he held up the Moracle in his right paw. Now they would see some theatre! He extended his other paw to the mob in the traditional fashion. It was claws in for life, claws out for death.

"Death! Death!" called the mob. Every claw was out.

"Death do you say?" Catligula replied. "So be it!"

With a practised flick of the paw, he flipped the Moracle high into the air. Letting go of the canvas, I dropped towards her. Captain Matro and his Spraetorians were almost upon Catligula. For a moment I thought that they would come in time. But even as I fell, I knew that Fortune's wheel had spun me a false one. The Moracle made no movement as she dropped into the Emperor's open jaws. Perhaps she had foreseen this? With a gulp, Catligula swallowed her whole.

WHITE NOISE

As I twisted to right myself in mid-fall, I heard a terrible high shriek – a cry of pain and anger. All who heard it fell to the floor, rolling in agony. Matro and his Spraetorians dropped their swords and buried their faces in the mud. They would have cut off their own ears to shut out that unbearable wail. The Great White Snake, who was making the sound, reared up high above Catligula. He thought only of the Moracle, now inside Catligula's body. The time had come for him to fulfil his purpose.

Catligula wound the remains of his costume around his head and stuffed it into his ears but he could not shut out that terrible noise. Still convinced of his godliness, he eyed the Great Snake in disgust. How dare this filthy creature spoil his performance? His last thought was that he would make the beast into a great white sofa for his bedroom.

The Great Snake opened its jaws, dislocating them to make them wider. Catligula was swallowed, almost lovingly. If the Great Snake's eyes had been able to register any expression, it would have been one of extreme satisfaction. His first purpose was now completed.

INSIDE OUT

The first thing I noticed on waking was a hissing noise. I was relieved to find that this was in fact a ringing noise in my ears, left behind when that terrible shrieking had gone. The next thing was the darkness and the stench of assorted rubbish. Someone had snuffed the sun out completely. There was an acrid smell, like burning. Dark shapes were pierced by two points of light. They began to glow and flicker. I made out the familiar face of Tefnut.

I was shaking. The Moracle had been eaten. The

Great Snake was loose in the world. We had failed. The ground began to tremble. Getting up and finding my balance, I saw that the sky was also shaking. It was as if the world had been turned upside down, inside out.

I began to mouth some questions but no words of sense came out.

"We are inside the belly of the Great Snake," said Tefnut, answering the question that I had not managed to ask.

"Swallowed?" I yowled in horror. "How can that be?"

"I tried to get you away but it was no use. We only made it this far."

She motioned for me to look up. Above me, I saw the outer wall of the Arena. I was lying in a drainage ditch – half full of water and rubbish. Under the rule of Catligula, the street sweepers and the other public servants had not been paid for months.

"But... But I thought you said we'd been swallowed. How did we escape?" I gasped.

"We didn't." she replied.

I struggled to make sense of what had happened. Catligula had swallowed the Moracle, then he himself had been swallowed by the Observer. The Great Snake had grown bigger and bigger until its shadow covered everything. How it had shrieked. Its noise was terrible. Someone had pulled me out of the ring and helped me towards an exit. That was as far as I got before another great shudder of ground and sky shook me.

"It is as I feared," said Tefnut.

"What?" I asked in horror.

"After he took Catligula, with the Moracle inside him, he grew and grew," she said bitterly. "As we were fleeing he must have swallowed the whole Arena. Now he will eat all the world."

"Doesn't he ever get full up?" I asked, forgetting that I'd been eaten for a moment.

"No," said Tefnut bitterly. "He grows as he eats. Then he sheds his skin."

How I wished that I could shed mine and slip away. But for all my wishing, I was stuck in it. Then I remembered the Moracle and the plot to kill Catligula. And all this because of the wretched 'witches' collar'.

"At least I can be rid of this now," I said, pawing at the buckle. But it would not move. I tugged at it again, but the harder I pulled, the tighter the collar became. I threw myself onto the ground, rolling and writhing but it was no use. It was cutting into my neck. Tefnut looked through me as I struggled.

"Why don't you help me!" I cried, exhausted.

Her eyes flickered.

"He is alive," she said.

When I'd stopped struggling, Tefnut explained that if Catligula were dead, the collar would have come off easily. The fact that it would not come off proved that the Emperor was still alive.

"We must be quick," she hissed. I had never heard her get excited like this before.

"Where is Catligula?" she demanded.

"I have no clue!" I replied, reminding her that neither of us had seen him since the Great Snake had eaten him.

"Remember what I told you," she hissed.

'Wherever you go, I will be,
Whatever you see, I can see,
Whenever I ...'

"Yes, yes. But I don't know how it works!" I protested.

"Close your eyes and think of nothing," said Tefnut.

"Yes," I said.

"Now think it, dream it. Where is Catligula?"

There was a pause. The ground shuddered and the sky rolled.

"I have no clue," I said.

"Be calm. Empty your mind," hissed Tefnut in a voice that could have been calmer.

"It's no use. I cannot think of nothing. It's hopeless. Now I'm thinking about thinking of nothing," I said in despair.

"Let your thoughts wander. Think about anything," said Tefnut.

The ground shuddered again. I did not know it, but we were passing further down into the belly of the snake.

"Be aware of your thoughts and tell me," she said.

"I was thinking about being eaten alive... The shame of it. Neferkitti and her father... The Moracle... Catligula."

And then it happened. Like the last time in the Moracle cave. I felt the collar tighten ever so slightly and a picture appeared on the inside lids of my closed eyes.

"Is he alive?" asked Tefnut.

"Yes... But in a dark place. There are bars... Cages... I can see – a white bull."

"Cages?" demanded Tefnut. The surprise in her voice drew me from the vision and I opened my eyes. The spell was broken. As soon as the floor stopped shaking, Tefnut started running.

TO THE VIVARIUM

As we ran I could hear a wailing from inside the Arena. The crowd had come to watch victories, for the spilling of blood and for the free fish. But now their world had been twisted and their sky had gone out. Their gods had forsaken them. Worse than forsaken – someone must have done something terrible, to anger the gods. Roman gods are either for you or against you, cross them and you will feel their teeth.

Tefnut led me along the outer wall and soon we reached a door used by servants to bring supplies into the auditorium. We twisted our way through the rubble and went downwards through a series of passages.

Every so often there was a terrible shaking that widened the cracks that were opening up in the walls and floor. There was a smell of panic in the air. Some of it was coming from me. But some of the fear about this place was older. Tefnut struggled with the door. With all my heart, I did not want to enter. I asked her where we were going. "Into the Vivarium" she answered.

As the Gladiators fight on the hot sand, they pay little attention to the world underneath their paws. The sand hides many secrets to add surprise to a fight to the death. Hidden under the Arena floor are traps and pits, great tanks for water, rooms full of machinery to lift the heavy scenery. There are some doors that even the most curious kitten would not dare to poke a whisker through. Some have never been opened since the Arena was built. Perhaps the strangest of all of these underground chambers is the Vivarium. It is from this underground zoo that the wild beasts emerge – as if by some act of the gods – and spring out onto the Arena floor. They give their lives in the beast hunts and gladiatorial displays. I thought of the thousands of beasts that had spent their final hours imprisoned here, ravenous in the dark. They'd hear the door click and walk unbelieving from their cages, making their way up through the tunnels towards the light and the air. But their freedom, like my own, would only be a brief run in the sunlight. Tefnut and I now stood at the door of this animal underworld. I heard a click. A well-oiled lock sprung open. And without another word, Tefnut disappeared into the darkness ahead of me.

DO NOT ENTER HERE

My heart still told me not to enter but I have learned to ignore her. I followed through the door and found myself in a corridor with chambers on both sides. The rooms had bars for doors and straw on the floor. 'Cages' was more like it except that only you could get a whole villa into some of them. Most were empty. The smell was very strong. Tefnut tasted the air again. Rather her than me!

"He is close," she said.

"Aren't I supposed to be the one who can tell that?" I said, stroking my collar.

"Listen," she whispered.

A sound halfway between a bellow and a roar rang down the corridor. Tefnut stalked towards a cage door, calling for me to follow.

"And you're sure he's in there?" I asked. I was at my bravest when I didn't have any time to think about it. We both peered through the bars into the chamber. "Come Mewpiter, don't be like that. We gods must get along you know," purred Catligula. He was sitting opposite an enormous white bull. The bull's polished horns were filed sharp. The Emperor turned god was no good at reading signals. First he had been swallowed whole. Soon after he had felt himself falling through endless darkness until at last he'd landed with a crash on what he'd assumed was Mount Olympuss — the home of the gods. The fall had left him dizzy and he'd wandered for a while until he had met the god Mewpiter, in the form of a white bull. But even in the afterlife, where he thought he was now, Catligula had to be the centre of attention. With a theatrical sweep he turned his back on the bull and examined the room, imagining all the changes he would make to Mount Olympuss. A lick of pea green paint would be the first thing.

"We have much to discuss brother," purred Catligula.

The bull snorted his disapproval. "Your palace, for a start. I never thought Mount Olympuss would be a dank old rat hole like this. You really should make more of an effort."

The bull scuffed the ground with his hoof and moved towards Catligula.

"And it smells like a cracked sewer," said Catligula rolling upon his stomach. He did not look well. "I'll be making some changes, now I am in charge," he announced. "I want my golden altar over there in the corner. You'll have to shift that old water trough of yours."

The bull, who had been raised on a farm in Cathens, not Mount Olympuss - had had enough. How dare this creature turn its back on him? He dropped his horns and charged the ruler of the Feline Empire. Catligula did not move a whisker. He would have been gored, but with a clang, the bull was pulled up short before his horns could find their mark. He was on the end of an iron chain, attached to a bar set into the stone on the far wall.

Catligula shook his head disapprovingly.

"Temper temper!" he said. "And mother always used to say that I was no good at sharing."

Horns down, the bull charged once more and was hauled up short again. He missed Catligula by a whisker. Returning to the far wall for another run, he scuffed his hooves in the dust and lowered his horns. The wall was weakening. One more charge would do it.

But what was this new annoyance? The bull noticed Tefnut as we might notice a flea. But what was this? The flea was dancing! Tefnut flowed from move to move, drawing the bull's attention away from his target. Everywhere she stepped, the dust rose upwards in perfect columns.

"Quickly!" she cried. I had been as distracted as the bull.

Carefully, I padded out towards the Emperor.

"Scribe?" called Catligula when he saw me. "So the Fleagyptians are right! We do get our old servants back, to serve us in the afterlife. What a pity! I should have had more of them killed before I died."

He rubbed his stomach. Now he looked as if he needed to lie down and eat a lot of grass.

"I could murder a decent cook for starters. I did have you killed, didn't I?" he asked.

"Caesar Best and Greatest, I have come with an

important message," I said.

"The Goddess Mewno wants to see you about setting up a new temple in your honour. She's waiting. Come this way!"

When I'd led him out of the cage, Tefnut followed us, leaving the dust to settle and the bull in peace.

ALL IS UNDONE

Out in the corridor, Tefnut glared at Catligula. His movements were slow. His belly was puffed out as if he had eaten something he shouldn't – which of course he had. He stared wide-eyed at Tefnut.

"Mewno?" he asked in a weak voice. "You don't look anything like you do in your statues."

Without fuss or theatricality, Tefnut extended her claws towards the Emperor's belly. They were long and filed sharper than the bull's horns. Catligula was now clutching at his stomach, in some pain. I realised what was coming next. Tefnut was planning a harsh cure for his stomach ache.

"Wait!" I cried. Not that way!"

Tefnut gave me a look that said "Why not?"

In truth I could not think of one good reason not to let Tefnut split Catligula in two right there and have done with it. Wasn't he a murderous tyrant, spoilt from the litter? That was what Matro had argued. Far away in the Vivarium, some injured beast let out a great howl, as if to underline this point. There was no good reason not to kill him, so I had to give a bad one.

"It's not right. Cutting him up like that," I hissed catching hold of Tefnut's paw.

Her eyes met mine and then fell to the collar around my neck.

"That," she said, "is the collar talking."

I had no time to consider what she meant by this. I was thinking about how unfair it would be to kill Catligula after going to all the trouble of finding him.

"You'll harm the Moracle," I added.

Shaking her head, Tefnut retracted her claws.

"How then?" she hissed.

"Please. Let me try," I asked. Pressing my nose almost up to Catligula's face, I said, "Caesar. Shall I escort you to the vomitorium?"

Tefnut watched, waiting for his reply.

"Yes. Better, go now," he said with a splutter.

We struggled into the next open cell we came to. It was empty, but there was a musty, jungle scent in it. I hoped this might help speed up what had to be done.

"Not even a bucket! These gods are a disgrace," said Catligula, clearly disappointed by the afterlife.

"Now Caesar don't grumble," I said in a matronly tone. Taking a deep breath, he threw his head forwards and started to choke. But it was a false hope.

His efforts came to nothing. After a minute trying to be sick, he looked sicker, but there was no result.

"By Mewpiter's crooked horns! It's no use! I can't do it!" he moaned.

Tefnut, who had been pacing the cell, began to

bristle. She stopped pacing and moved towards the two of us.

"Come on now. That's the way. Better out than in!" I cried in desperation.

"After this we'll go to the Goddess Mewno's banquet. She'll have lots of tasty treats lined up for a mighty God like you. There'll be double stuffed swans on a bed of raw cod eggs... "

Catligula lurched forward.

"Green river eels, still with their slime on... "

Catligula's eyes bulged.

"Lots of mussels, with their sweet sticky seaweedy beards. And live white mice for afters."

With an indescribable cry Catligula lurched forward and the contents of his stomach broke like a wave on the floor of the cell. With no fear of the stench, Tefnut began to paw through the mess. She emerged carrying a limp white body in her mouth. With gentle care she began to lick it. This was true devotion.

After a moment she looked up, excited. There was a spark in there – a twitch of the whiskers. The Moracle rolled over and sat up.

"She lives! Mewpiter be praised!" I cried.

Tefnut did not join the celebration.

"What's the matter? What has happened?" I asked.

"Nothing has happened," she replied.

"That is the trouble. The Moracle lives but nothing has happened. It is as I feared. What has been done cannot be undone." She looked like she had lost a real mouse and found a toy one.

"What did you expect?" said a voice inside my head. It was too high pitched to be taken seriously. "We are still inside the Observer," thought the Moracle.

Gently, Tefnut scooped up the Moracle in her mouth. And without a second glance at Catligula, she ran from the room.

REALLY FREE

I looked at the ruler of the known world. His beautiful coat was a disgrace. But he looked rather pleased with himself now that he had done what he'd come to do.

"Water! By Neptuna bring it quickly." he commanded.

His thin eyes flicked about the room. He didn't look like a god, or an emperor anymore. Something about him was different. Then I saw that in his haste to relieve himself, he had taken off his golden collar.

"Quickly!" hissed Tefnut.

"What?" I asked.

Carefully, Tefnut placed the Moracle on the ground and began to undo my collar. There was no tightening or choking. In a moment it was undone and I held it in my paw.

"I will take that," said Tefnut, unclipping the gold coin at the centre before throwing the collar away.

On the way back, I stopped and unhooked the white bull's chain from the wall. I was free again. Everyone else should have their chance. As for Catligula, he would have to take his. His flame didn't seem as bright anymore. When dawn comes, the moths stop flying for the moon.

INSIDE OUT

With great speed we wound our way upward. As we climbed higher, the ground shook with increasing force. The atmosphere was choking, all dust and dead things. How I longed to run free in the sunlight. I forgot the fact that I cannot stand the strong sun, and that I never run unless I have a very good reason. As we pushed through the broken door, I remembered my problems. The darkness had silenced the crowd inside the Arena, save for the occasional cries. I put a paw into something sticky and cried out. All around me, the ground was covered in a clear film.

"It is shed snake skin," said Tefnut. "He is growing."

"Urrgh!" I hissed, wiping my paw. "It's all over the place. But what's it doing in here?"

"He eats everything. He wants the whole world inside his belly," she replied.

"But eating your own skin," I hissed. "That's disgusting!"

"I know a cat who loves the taste of his own claw clippings," said a voice inside my head. Shamed, I said nothing. There was no disputing with the Moracle.

Tefnut sat and stared out into the thin air in that peculiar way of hers, as if she was asleep with her eyes open. Whilst the world span around her she was the calm centre, the hub of the turning wheel. I wanted to do something. We had to get the Moracle outside. But surely the Great Snake wasn't going to let us just walk out of his jaws? Someone had to think of something.

"Oh Great Moracle," I thought, "can I ask you a question?"

"Not that question," thought the Moracle. "It is against the Seer's Code for me to make prophesies about my own fate."

"Then what in the name of Peus are we going to do?" I hissed. There was silence.

"We can't just sit here!" I shouted.

I kicked the ground and a cloud of dust flew up into Tefnut's eyes. She turned towards me.

"What would you suggest?" she asked.

"We could climb up to the mouth," I said.

"We would climb for miles," she replied.

"We could try," I said.

"It would not work. Snakes' teeth point backwards, to keep their prey inside," she explained.

"Well we could claw our way out, through the nose."

"Impossible," said Tefnut shaking her head. I learned that a snake's 'nose' does not connect with its mouth. How wise Tefnut was. And how annoying! Apparently, she knew everything except how to get us out of this.

"Well we could light a fire, and get the snake to spit us out," I said triumphantly.

Tefnut began to quote. "The Great Snake will eat

all the fires. He will drink all the seas. He will eat and eat..."

"Yes, yes, he will eat and eat until he has eaten all the world. You've said that already," I hissed.

"Please!" I begged. "You're the mystic. Summon up a great eagle and fly us out!"

Tefnut said nothing, waiting for the storm to pass. But there is nothing like a cool silence to make anger hotter.

"We've been swallowed. Do something!" I hissed, kicking a cloud of dust towards her.

Her great eyes opened wide.

"Spartapuss. When there is really nothing you can do, it is better to do nothing," she said.

I sat down, growling at myself.

"Good," said Tefnut. "Now we will wait, for nature to take her course."

EVERYTHING MUST PASS

When Fortune spins us a new thread, how quickly we get used to it. I feel the sun on my coat, warming me. I hear the birds' songs, annoying me. All the time, we are moving onwards but we do not notice it. In a small ship, you cannot see the tide running.

Even as I was shouting, the Arena, the Moracle and all had been passing down though the great body of the snake. And the snake grew and grew as time passed, until we became as small as fleas, as small as dust. And we travelled through the belly of the snake.

And in the end, we were passed from the other end, Moracle and all. It took some time.

BAD TO WORSE

In my experience whenever you think things cannot get worse, they invariably do. The embarrassment of being swallowed alive was hard to bear, but it was nothing compared to the unmentionable shame of travelling through the snake's gut and down its inside passages and being toileted out undigested.

Tefnut, the Moracle and I alone had to bear this shame. As soon as we had been passed – and the Moracle was outside the snake's belly, the process was reversed. The Great Snake shrank, spitting out all that he had swallowed. The outside was the outside again. And Romans in the Arena wept for joy, thanking their gods for saving them. They might have cheered their Emperor too – but he was nowhere to be found.

ONE MORE SPIN

Amongst the joy and songs of celebration, one amongst us looked uneasy, as if new dangers were everywhere.

"Tefnut, what's wrong?" I asked.

She gave me a look as if to say - "What do you think?"

"Oh no," I sighed. "You are about to tell me that we are all in terrible danger because of some new ancient curse or a prophecy or something of that nature."

She did not reply. Her look said it all.

"In Peus' name! Can't we have a moment being happy to be alive again?" I asked.

"There is something I must do," she replied.

"Surely you're not thinking of going near that snake again, are you? That would be madness."

"I must find the Observer and delay him. But I must also return the Moracle to her cave. When she is in her cave, we will be safe. If she leaves the cave, the Observer follows her."

A thought crossed my mind – that I would like to be safe in a cave myself – or up a tree even – anywhere but here with a Great Snake on the slither that had eaten all the world and might want seconds.

"You look for the snake, and I'll take the Moracle back to her cave," I said. Tefnut's big eyes flickered. There was reason in my argument and so she agreed.

REPURRBLIC! REPURRBLIC!

The journey to the cave was a long one, so I got hold of a comfortable little box for the Moracle and I bought her some seeds. And for myself, a dormouse kebab, roasted to perfection and served with fish liquor. I was considering a little sleep before starting out. Then I remembered my promise to Tefnut and decided to get it over with. We were making good progress down the Mewlian Way, when I was stopped by some Spraetorians.

"Halt! State your name and your business," growled the lead guard.

But before I could answer, a wiry figure said:

"You're his scribe intcha?"

"His scribe! His scribe!" hissed another voice.

They crowded around me.

"Get his name!" said a guard with a list.

"I'm Spartapuss," I said. "And I'm sure there has been some misunderstanding."

"Kill him! Death take 'em all!" screamed the small tabby excitedly.

"Repurrblic, Repurrblic!" cried another.

The big Scenturian who was in charge rolled his eyes and flicked his tail.

"For Peus' sake! Stop shouting out the secret watchword to every stray we meet," he growled.

"Sir! Sir! Let's take him back and terror gate 'im," said the small one.

"Do what?" said the Scenturian.

"Terror gate 'im. Put him in the terror gate. Like we does with spies, Scent."

"It's in-terr-o-gate him, you rat dropping!" spat the Scenturian.

"By Neptuna's pointy fork, you lot are the dimmest troops in the western legions. Half of you need a recipe to boil water."

The group said nothing. They knew not to say anything when the Scent was off on one of his rants. Finally, someone asked for permission to speak.

Permission was granted. My saviour was Patchus, the old guard I had met up the cedar tree, in the

Imperial Gardens.

"Me and Spartapuss goes back a long way, Sir. We escaped from the Purrmanians together. They had us both up a tree."

"Bring him along," ordered the Scenturian. Not again, I thought.

HIDE CLAWDIUS

As we marched towards the palace, I could find very little to be thankful for. I was used to being blind-folded. And at least they had not taken time to search me. The Moracle would be the first thing that they'd find. It was clear that being Catligula's scribe was no longer a good thing to be. And if it was a bad time to be a favourite of the Emperor, it was a terrible time to be a relation. The Clawdian family tree was about to be felled, limb by limb.

As we neared the palace gates, the Scenturian called us to a halt.

"Right lads," he began, remembering his doctor's advice and not shouting, for a change. "Here's where we earn ourselves some extra pension. I want you all searching in twos, and if you find one of 'em, shout out for help and be ready for a fight. They'll know what our game is soon enough."

"What about the prisoner Sir?" said the nasty little tabby.

"You and Patchus, take him down the guard house and lock him up tight."

"Can't we kill 'im now and get our rewards?" said tabby. The Scenturian sighed.

"The reward is for family members only. There's twenty in gold per tail for every dead Clawdian. But he ain't family."

"And go carefully lads," said the Scenturian. "There's some big Purrmanians about what's still loyal to the old Emperor. If you see any – give it the signal."

And with that he sprang off towards the palace, with rest of them following behind. An unexpected pounce knocked me over. I fell face down in the dirt.

"Hold still! There's no call for that!" said Patchus.

"It int fair!" hissed the tabby.

"What now?" said Patchus, wearily.

"Everyone else is on the hunt but we've got to 'scort this stray back to the guard house."

"They tells us something. We does it. It's called orders. You hear a lot of it in the army." said Patchus.

"But they'll get all the rewards for themselves!" he whined.

"Not necessarily," I said.

"How come?" he asked.

"Well your Scenturian has taken the rest of them over to search the Imperial Apartments. But if you were a Clawdian, where would you be hiding?"

There was silence.

"I dunno. I'm not a dirty Clawdian," spat the tabby, giving me a dig with his sword.

"Go on," said Patchus.

"Well, it seems a shame that you've got to take me straight to the prison. I mean, if you had an experienced guide, someone who knows every corner of the palace..."

The two of them discussed my offer. Soon I was blinking in the sunlight, for a blindfolded guide is no use to anyone. Looking at Patchus' thin black face, I saw that the white patch over his left eye was looking a bit threadbare. The old soldier was tough as iron claws but he had a weary look about him, as if he really was ready to start drawing his pension.

"Sorry about this Spartapuss. Order's is orders. But if you could see your way to helping out, well you know I'd use my influence and do everything to see you right."

My heart leapt. Good old Patchus! I wondered if an escape could be arranged.

"Put you down for the easiest torturer. Make sure they don't do nothing in your water. That sort of thing," he promised.

My heart stopped leaping. It seemed as if another plan would be in order.

"Where do we start?" asked Patchus.

I led them through the kitchen towards the guest apartments. The further inside we got, the more exotic the designs became. It was a sea of pea green paint and Squeak marble.

"Where now?" asked Patchus.

I started down the corridor, thinking that we may as well search anywhere. So I stepped over a 'Welcome' mosaic into the first room we came to. There was a familiar smell about the place.

"Here's a good place to start," I said, pointing towards a stone archway. Excited, the nasty little tabby sprang through the arch.

Unknown to me, it led to the guest toilet. The nasty little tabby wasn't impressed. He struck me in the face with the flat of his sword. Patchus growled at him.

"What? He had it coming to 'im!" whined the tabby, backing off.

"Do you want to find any Clawdians or not? They know we're out to kill 'em. We're not going to stroll in and find 'em reclining on their lovely sofa reading Cato! We're going to have to search," he said.

He began to tear the place apart and tabby joined in. Furniture went flying, tables were turned, cushions were scattered. In moments, the room looked like a battlefield.

"Nothing," said Patchus.

"Purrmanians' bits!" shouted the tabby, throwing his sword at the last remaining piece of unbroken pottery, a fine Squeak urn.

It shattered and a cloud of ashes filled the room. I covered my mouth, for it is not polite to breathe in someone's dead relation.

From behind the curtain at the back of an alcove,

there came a muffled sneeze. My heart fell like a kitten down a well.

The nasty little tabby waved his sword.

"Who's there?" said Patchus to the curtain.

"Give yourself up and we'll make it easy on you!" he added. The tabby got ready to strike.

With a swish, Patchus drew back the curtain. There, crouching on the top shelf of the cupboard on a pile of linen was Clawdius.

"Spartapuss?" he cried, astonished.

The nasty little tabby sprang back in panic, as if he had just come nose to nose with one of his dead ancestors.

Clawdius backed further into the corner, but there was nowhere to go.

"Come down!" said the tabby waving his sword in excitement. "We ain't ere to 'urt you!"

"Who are you?" asked Patchus.

"He's nobody important," I said. "Just an old servant."

But Patchus wasn't fooled.

"Get down here now!" he ordered.

Clawdius leapt down from the alcove, landing badly on his weak back legs.

"Hang about!" said Patchus. "You're the lame uncle with the stutter. The one the Emperor was always making fun of."

"I don't suppose the g-great joker is laughing now. But I'd wager that Captain Matro and my wife have got a s-smile on their faces," said Clawdius.

"Ain't you meant to be an arf wit?" said the nasty little tabby.

Patchus laughed.

"There's your answer. Things are not always as they first appear," I said.

"Well Sir, I'm truly sorry that it has to be like this," said Patchus. "But our orders are to leave no members of the Imperial Family alive. But seeing as you is noble and of high breeding and all, I'll tell you what we'll do. We'll leave you now, and you can start your 'last march' yourself, if you take my meaning. But we can only step out for a minute mind."

"And if you don't 'ave the guts to do it," began the nasty little tabby, "We'll have to come back and kill..."

"Assist you Sir, if you get my meaning," said Patchus.

"Yes, q-quite plainly," said Clawdius, with a little splutter.

"Nothing personal. We're doing it all for the Purrblic!" said the tabby.

"He means for The Repurrblic Sir," explained Patchus.

Clawdius laughed. He was sure now that the gods had a good sense of humour. He had long been a Repurrblican himself, in secret. He once told me that years of living with a family as bad as his own would be enough to turn anyone against the Emperors.

"Well, this is a very kind gesture Spraetorian. I appreciate it," said Clawdius.

"He's always got on with the army," I said, trying to think of some ending, other than this.

"Perhaps you remember his brother Purrmanipuss?" I added. Patchus looked up. Everyone loved Purrmanipuss.

"I had the pleasure of serving under your brother Sir. At the Neuterberger Forest. Best commander you could wish for."

"Yes," said Clawdius with a slight crack in his voice. "He was the b-best b-brother you could wish for."

Patchus tail dropped. This was a harsh spin of Fortune's wheel but his orders were clear.

"Well, Sir" he said saluting Clawdius, "We'll just step out now. And leave you to it." Warily, the little tabby put his sword down on the floor and followed Patchus out of the room.

"Clawdius, I am sorry," I began.

He shook his head.

"Save that speech Spartapuss, it is not for this world. But do me one more g-g-good service if you will, for the sake of times past." And he gave me the blade to hold steady.

HISTORY

The wife of the great philosopher Cato once said that cats have nine lives. Old Cato had the brain the size of an island. He was the cleverest thinker, spending all day working out the answers to difficult questions of philosophy and doing his accounts. But he was a devil at night. As soon as the sun was down he'd be up prowling about the rooftops of Cathens. He'd out-stare and out-shout every other tom in the city. There were complaints about his yowls from the town of Furbes, ten miles away. His wife became sick of him. He'd been out for eight nights in a row when she came up with the idea that every cat has 'nine lives' and told him very firmly that he'd used up a life for each night on the tiles. Now he'd got to life number nine, so he'd better start behaving himself, or there would be big trouble.

But old Cato was proud as well as stubborn and ignored her warning. Two days later he was killed in a spear-fishing accident. It is said that it was his wife who arranged for the assassination, making sure to have the spear poisoned with the venom of a rare octopus, which kills in less than three seconds. He lived to the age of thirteen years old, which is now said to be a very unlucky number.

I'm going into the history of old Cato because I have been offered a job as a historian at the palace. This has been a most lucky spin from Fortune's wheel. I do not yet know which god historians use, so today I shall sacrifice to the Goddess as usual.

I confess that I have very little experience but as far as I can see, the difference between writing your own diary and writing a history book is that writing a history is harder because you have to make a lot of things up where there are no facts available. For example, I do not know if the great Philosopher Cato, who I mentioned earlier, was actually a devil at night or not. But I imagine that he would have been a devil because writing all of that philosophy all day must have had him climbing the walls. Also I do not know for sure that he was killed by a spear, or that his wife ordered his death or that he was thirteen when he died. I know only that he was a philosopher. And I expect he was married.

As you can see I shall have my work cut out for me at the palace and I'll certainly need to use my imagination. So I will start with imagining what happened out in the corridor, where Patchus and the nasty little tabby were waiting for Clawdius to take his own life.

THE WARDROBE

Patchus knew that there was something wrong as soon as he stepped out into the corridor and heard the heavy tread of big cats running towards him. He didn't need to wait to hear their battle cries. He knew Purrmanian Bodyguards when he heard them. And these Purrmanians were not in a good mood, for the body they had been guarding was missing, presumed dead.

Since they had nobody else to guard, revenge had to be taken and they would take it wherever they could find it. As soon as the sun had come back, and their war god Klaws had got a grip in the afterworld, and delivered his tribe back safe, Dogren and his cohort had had only one thought. To find the traitors – the oath breakers – the Emperor's murderers – and make them wish they had been drowned at birth.

But when the Purrmanians turned the corner, Patchus saw that they were hard on the heels of another group. It was The Scenturian and the rest of the lads. The Purrmanians were outnumbered, but when Bodyguards go berserk, numbers don't count.

Patchus sprang back into the room, disturbing Clawdius, who was greatly annoyed. He hadn't even had the chance to say his prayers yet.

"Spraetorian! G-give me a m-minute more please," he spluttered.

"Sorry Sir but there's a lot of Purrmanians out there going berserk. It's every cat for himself!"

"Kill 'im now! Before them Purrmanians gets our reward," said the nasty little tabby.

Patchus gave him a hard stare.

"That would not be a good idea," I said.

In burst the big Scenturian and the rest of Spraetorians. Without a second glance at us they wedged the door shut and began to pile furniture in front of it. I leapt up onto a shelf and called for Clawdius to do the same.

Carefully, I took out the box containing the Moracle and opened the lid. The Moracle's pink eyes blinked and her whiskers twitched as she gazed up at us.

"Oh great Moracle, what can I do now?" I asked.

"Silence," thought the Moracle, "I must speak with the Emperor. Clawdius, come closer for I have an important prophecy for you. You will travel to the land of the Kittons and there you will…"

I closed the box before the Moracle had finished her prophecy because I'd had an idea. Every last piece of furniture was now in front of the door, and the Spraetorians had their full weight on it.

I drew myself up to my full height.

"Listen, everyone," I cried. Nobody listened. I tried to get the attention of the big Scenturian. The door shook on its hinges.

"They're charging the door!" came a cry. Actually the Purrmanians hadn't started charging – they were just trying it.

"Listen!" I cried again. "This is Clawdius, Catligula's uncle, the brother of the great Purrmanipuss. Take a good look at him because he's going to be your new Emperor."

The Scenturian stared at me in wonder. The little tabby laughed as if it was the funniest thing he'd ever heard.

"I'm serious," I continued. "When the Purrmanians come in here, they'll want a fight. But they won't be getting one. Because – we're going to give them an Emperor to guard!"

"What about us? It's our job to guard the palace!" said the Scenturian.

"Exactly!" I said. "And where do you think you'll be with The Senate in charge of a Repurrblic? There won't be a palace. You Spraetorians need an Emperor more than anyone."

The room shuddered. The oak door began to splinter and crack. The Spraetorians threw themselves against it to try to keep it shut. From the corridor, a low voice called:

"Open up! Or it will go badly for you."

The big Scenturian looked from the door to Clawdius, shaking his head.

"What about the Purrblic?" asked a high voice.

"That tabby has fur for brains," thought the Scenturian, "order him to kill a fish and he'd try to drown it!

"I'd keep quiet about The Repurrblic if I were you," gasped Patchus, throwing his full weight against the door. "The Purrmanians have never cared for The Repurrblic. Isn't that right Scent?"

The Scenturian nodded.

"But why 'ave that old fool for an Emperor?" said the tabby.

"It ain't the cat, it's the pedigree that's the thing," said Patchus. "He's the last of the Clawdian line. And he's brave too. Didn't even twitch when I offered him the knife just now. He even thanked me for it."

There was another impact and the door shattered into pieces.

Only a wardrobe stood between us and the loyal Purrmanians.

"He's the best candidate for Emperor you'll find in this room!" I shouted.

"But what if I don't want to be your Emperor?" asked Clawdius, without faltering this time.

"Of course you do Caesar. It's better than having a dagger stuck in yer insides Sir," said the Scenturian with a smile. And he hoisted Rome's reluctant new ruler onto his shoulders, cushion and all.

"Come on lads," said the Scenturian. "Sing out loud for your new Caesar. Good old Clawdius!"

And so it was that when the Purrmanian Bodyguards broke into the room ready for their bloody revenge, the first thing they saw was an old grey cat sitting on the big Scenturian's back, newly crowned with a wreath of flowers. And the shout that rang in their ears and all through Rome was: "Hail Clawdius! Hail Caesar, Best and Greatest!"

The Official History of the Emperor Clawdius as told to his historian Spartapuss by the Best and Greatest one himself

All Rome celebrated alongside their new Emperor today on the happy occasion of his divorce from his second wife Mogullania. The event has gripped the public imagination and all over Rome unhappy couples are splitting up. The court heard how Mogullania had joined a conspiracy to murder her husband. No date for her trial has been set. During the hearing, the Emperor was guarded by a joint force of Purrmanian Bodyguards and Spraetorians led by the acting Chief of Security – Dogren of Purrmania.

At a reception after the trial the Emperor was joined by a group of close personal friends and well-wishers. They had a splendid feast at the admission price of just three gold coins per head. Special coins have been struck to celebrate the divorce and are available at all official souvenir outlets.

CATILIS X

July 10th

Equal Fights

I HAVE JUST RETURNED from the Emperor's divorce celebrations, which I was pleased to attend with Katrin and Russell. A group of senators crowded around the Emperor Clawdius. He was trying to convince them that they should get rid of Emperors and bring back The Repurrblic but they weren't having any of it. He knows he is stuck with the job. I think he is getting used to the idea now that he can see the financial benefits but he has a lot to learn. I caught Dogren explaining to the Emperor that he should stop saying 'Please' and 'Thank you' to his guards. Apparently it's bad for their morale. It was nice to see the Purrmanians and Spraetorians taking it in turns to guard Clawdius. The Spraetorians are to have a new Captain but Matro's successor has not been named yet. Clawdius has asked the Spraetorians themselves to come up with a list of names! He told me that he could forgive Captain Matro for leading a revolt against Catligula and plotting with his wife, but not for ordering the guards to destroy the Clawdian family.

During the dinner, Neferkitti approached me with a smile.

"You can tell your sister that the Moracle is safely back in her house," I said.

"Tefnut sends her thanks, for everything you have done," she replied.

High above, in the roof of the hall, two plump sparrows fought viciously over a piece of straw.

"It is lucky that birds don't have claws," said Neferkitti.

Spring had arrived and it was time for all of that nest building and feathering. Speaking of which, I heard that our new Emperor had received three marriage proposals already.

Neferkitti threw back her head to get a better view

of the sparrow fight.

I couldn't help noticing her collar. The design was like a smaller version of the 'witches' collar' that Catligula and I had worn. Again I wondered how something so small could cause so much trouble.

"I'd take that coin off your collar if I were you," I said. "Who knows what sort of trouble it could lead to?"

Neferkitti looked shocked. Had I said something offensive?

"I can't take it off, for I am married," she said.

"I'm terribly sorry, I had no idea. About the collar, I mean. No one ever told me…" I said.

"We Fleagyptians are not like you Romans – getting married and divorced and then marrying again at the flick of a tail. Once the marriage collar is on, it is on for life," said Neferkitti in earnest.

"I see," I replied, trying to think of some way to change the subject.

"But we are very liberal now," laughed Neferkitti. "In the olden days they made strong collars, with a real pull. My grandmother used to say that you knew who was the master, as soon as you were wearing one of them."

Then a terrible thought occurred to me.

"What did they look like, these old collars?" I said.

And to my horror she replied:

"Like mine – only bigger. They came in matching

sets. The males of course would wear the biggest one. And once the collars were on, the romance would be over and the female's work would start. Always it would be obey, obey, obey!"

"For Peus' sake!" I said, "And what if you didn't want to obey?"

"Then you would feel it. Tight around the throat!" She made a choking sound.

"And there would be no sneaking away either. Your other half would discover it. We have a saying: 'Wherever you go, I will be. Whatever you see, I can see...'"

The remains of my rat kebab fell from my mouth, leaving a dark stain on the white floor. I felt as if I had a lot in common with Neferkitti's grandmother.

"Surely you don't still allow that now?" I gasped, horrified.

"No. Not any more," laughed Neferkitti. "The law was changed before I was born."

High above us the two sparrows were still locked in battle over their very important piece of straw. Neither would give way. They beat their tiny wings and fluttered for their lives and they tugged for the prize. But it was a dead heat, with neither bird gaining ground over the other.

"Everything is equal these days," laughed Neferkitti, pointing at the birds. "It causes less trouble, in the end."

I AM SPARTAPUSS

By Robin Price

In the first adventure in the Spartapuss series...
Rome AD 36. The mighty Feline Empire rules the world.
Spartapuss, a ginger cat is comfortable managing Rome's
finest Bath and Spa. But Fortune has other plans for him.
Spartapuss is arrested and imprisoned by Catligula, the
Emperor's heir. Sent to a school for gladiators, he must
fight and win his freedom in the Arena - before his oppo-
nents make mouse-meat out of him.

'This witty Roman romp is history with cattitude.'
Junior Magazine (Scholastic)

ISBN 10: 09546576-0-8
ISBN 13: 978-0-9546576-0-4

UK £6.99
USA $14.95/ CAN $16.95

For USA/ Canada orders contact:
Independent Publishers Group
Phone: 312.337.0747
FAX: 312.337.5985
http://www.ipgbook.com/

Download free Spartapuss wallpaper at
www.mogzilla.co.uk

DIE CLAWDIUS

By Robin Price

The most gripping adventure yet in the acclaimed Spartapuss series...

Clawdius, the least likely Emperor in Roman history, needs to show his enemies who is boss. So he decides to invade Spartapuss' home – The Land of the Kitons. As battle lines are drawn, Spartapuss must take sides. Can the magic of the Mewids help him to save the day?

ISBN 09546576-8-3
978-0-9546576-8-0

UK £6.99 (paperback)
USA $14.95 / CAN $16.95

For USA / Canada orders contact:
Independent Publishers Group
Phone: 312.337.0747
FAX: 312.337.5985
http://www.ipgbook.com/

Download free Spartapuss wallpaper at www.mogzilla.co.uk

COUNT MILKULA

A tale of milk and monsters

By Woodrow Phoenix & Robin Price

Lemmy's world is rocked when he loses his bedroom to his
new baby brother. So he turns to Granny for comfort and a
bedtime story. She tells the tale of Count Milkula, a selfish,
noisy, milk-crazed creature from the monotonous mountains
of Mamsylvania. Lemmy finds out that, like baby brothers,
Mampires can't do anything for themselves. That's why
looking after them is such an adventure.

For ages 5 and up
32 pages
Full colour illustrations

ISBN 0-9546576-5-9 • 978-0-9546576-5-9
Hardback: UK £11.99 USA $22.95 CAN $24.95

ISBN 0-9546576-6-7 • 978-0-9546576-6-6
Paperback: UK £5.99 USA $14.95 CAN $16.95

For USA / Canada orders contact:
Independent Publishers Group
Phone: 312.337.0747
FAX: 312.337.5985
http://www.ipgbook.com/

SANTA CLAUS IS ON A DIET

By Nancy Scott-Cameron & Craig Conlan

Mrs Claus looked Santa up and down
She shook her head, began to frown
'Santa dearest, the problem's that
in plain words darling,
you're too fat!'

With narrow chimneys now a danger, Mrs Claus decides that it's time for Santa to cut down on calories. The reindeer, keen to lighten their load, are only too happy to help. But there's a fatal flaw in their weight loss plan. Is Santa on a crash diet?

For ages 4 and up
32 pages • Full colour illustrations
Available: 01/09/07

ISBN 09546576-9-1 • 978-0-9546576-9-7
Paperback: UK £5.99 USA $14.95 CAN $16.95

For USA / Canada orders contact:
Independent Publishers Group
Phone: 312.337.0747
FAX: 312.337.5985
http://www.ipgbook.com/

ABOUT THE AUTHOR

Robin Price was born in Wantage in 1968. Before going to work in Japan, Robin left his cat, Bleep, with his mum and dad. When he returned, Bleep was as fat as a barrel. His parents had followed the instructions on the cat food: 'Feed your cat as much as it can eat. Cats regulate their own diet and seldom overeat'.

I Am Spartapuss is Robin's first novel. The sequel, *Catligula,* was published in 2005. His third novel, *Die Clawdius* was published in 2006.